New England's Haunted Lighthouses

Ghostly Legends and Maritime Mysteries

Allan Wood

New England's Haunted Lighthouses:
Ghostly Legends and Maritime Mysteries

Paperback: ISBN 979-8-9888241-2-1

Dedication

This book is dedicated in memory to my parents and their unwavering support in every endeavor or project I have chosen. It is also dedicated to those lighthouse keepers, Coast Guardsmen, caretakers, service members, and community members, both past and present, who risked their lives to assist those in danger—whether out of duty or because they believed it was the right thing to do. Thank you. This book is also dedicated to honoring those who have passed before us, and may their spirits rest in peace either here on earth or above.

Acknowledgments

Most images in this book are my own creations as the author, with proper credit given for those sourced from the public domain. I want to thank the Coast Guard, the U.S. Lighthouse Service, the Library of Congress Prints and Photographs Division, and Wikipedia for allowing me to use their images freely. I also want to express my gratitude to my wife, Chris, for her support, and to my sons, Bryan, and Steven, for keeping me inspired and grounded.

Contents

Introduction

New England is rich with ghost stories and folklore. Many of these fascinating tales originate from real events, leading to credible accounts of paranormal activities or sightings from various reliable sources, including locals, tourists, mariners, officers, and lighthouse keepers. For centuries, lighthouses have stood as solitary sentinels, enduring storms and bearing witness to the passage of time. It's no surprise that these beacons have inspired numerous legends and stories, merging maritime history with the paranormal.

Many lighthouses were established in remote locations, often overwhelming the keepers and their families. This sometimes resulted in tragic illnesses or suicides, later reported as ghost sightings after their deaths. Some keepers fell victim to foul play, were killed in tragic accidents, or were caught in New England's fierce storms. Some keepers were so devoted to their lighthouse stations that their spirits lingered after death to ensure the beacon was well-maintained. Numerous lighthouse stations have been the sites of nearby shipwrecks or were located near quarantine stations for the sick, where many souls perished, contributing to reports of paranormal events.

This book, featuring black-and-white images of each lighthouse, describes various sightings and events at or near these landmarks along the New England coast. It includes historical accounts that enhance the understanding of these paranormal occurrences. Brief tidbits of the history of these lighthouses offer context for their locations. These narratives aim to explain why certain events may have occurred and how some stories became part of New England folklore. Additionally, many factual accounts remain unexplained, handed down through the years by respected individuals. Professional paranormal investigators have scrutinized several of these lighthouses to verify and substantiate claims made by others, and their findings are included as well. These tales highlight not only ghosts and spirits but also the histories of individuals who lived and worked at these stations or who were shipwrecked nearby, intertwining their lives with the sea and the supernatural.

Haunted Lighthouses in Connecticut

Connecticut's rocky shoreline, stretching from Greenwich to Stonington, with its treacherous ledges, shoals, and islands along Fisher's Island Sound and Long Island Sound, constantly kept mariners on alert, claiming the lives of many during New England's fierce storms. Lighthouses were constructed to protect mariners from these dangerous rocky areas and guide them into some of Connecticut's busiest harbors during the height of the whaling, fishing, and tourist industries that thrived in the nineteenth century.

Several lighthouses built in southwestern Connecticut are situated on perilous rock islands or ledges. Some lighthouses in the region were designed as unique stone structures and are often referred to as the "Castles of the Sound." One of these structures, located on Sheffield Island, is believed to be haunted by strange music and other phenomena. Another beacon was erected on Penfield Reef, infamous for being one of the most treacherous ledges in Long Island Sound, haunted by a keeper who drowned but is still helping mariners.

Additionally, lighthouses were constructed in the Stratford Harbor area due to frequent foggy conditions. One such lighthouse stands on the dangerous Stratford Shoal, said to be haunted by an assistant keeper who went insane. New London Harbor also experiences persistent fog. The perilous New London Ledge marks the harbor entrance, with its distinctive brick lighthouse rumored to be haunted by a ghost nicknamed "Ernie," and possibly other spirits.

Strange Noises and Music

Sheffield Island Light, Norwalk, Connecticut

Several lighthouses built in southwestern Connecticut were located on perilous rock islands or ledges to guide vessels into the bustling harbors of Norwalk and Stamford along Long Island Sound. Norwalk Harbor, surrounded by sixteen islands, became a significant hub for oyster production in the nineteenth century, hosting one of the largest oyster beds in the world. Sheffield Island, the second-largest island in this distinctive group, is home to one of those uniquely designed stone beacons known as the "Castles of the Sound." It was built in 1826 to signal the treacherous islands along the entrance to Norwalk Harbor.

Stone architecture of Sheffield Island Lighthouse.

Sheffield Island and the lighthouse are marked by their own peculiar tragedy. In July 1872, Keeper Noah Mosher, who had assumed the position in 1861, was observing vessels pass through his spyglass while talking with visitors in the dining room. Suddenly, he stopped, leaned back, clutched his chest, and died, much to the horror of his guests.

Before the lighthouse was built and even during its operation, shipwrecks continued to occur. Some reports describe unusual music, sounds of footsteps on the second floor of the lighthouse or up the stairs, and cries for help. This was further supported in 1991 when archaeologist Karen Orawsky was investigating a historic area of the island. One day, while approaching the island in a boat, she heard "hypnotic and mystical" music emanating from the island but could not determine its source. She also noted hearing a faint foghorn out on the water along with distant cries for help, with no one in sight. Over the years, others who have cared for the island have reported hearing these strange sounds. Condè Nast Traveler, a lifestyle travel magazine, recognized Sheffield Island and its lighthouse as one of the 32 most "haunted" places in the United States.

Despite the many tourists visiting the island yearly, reports of ghost sightings or strange sounds remain infrequent. However, a team of eighteen paranormal investigators, led by Christine Kaczynski, founder of the Connecticut Paranormal Research and Investigations organization, was called to the island. No information was provided to allow for unbiased scrutiny. A psychic was also brought along as part of the team. They utilized specialized equipment to measure electronic voice phenomena (EVPs), specialized temperature gauges to identify cold spots, infrared cameras, and other types of recording and sound equipment to measure and record any abnormalities around the lighthouse. Their findings suggested that the lighthouse may be home to three spirits, including a young girl named Abby, who was about seven years old when she perished. All three entities seem to be trapped on the island. They contacted the girl spirit on the second floor of the stone lighthouse. They believed one of the other entities may be a former keeper (Keeper Noah Mosher?).

The reports of unusual music might be linked to the island's namesake and original owner, Captain Robert Sheffield, who sold the land to the government to build the lighthouse. He had a unique talent for musical instruments and loved playing different types. The Captain was known for playing a distinctive instrument from traditional 19th century Iceland, called the langspil, which resembles an oversized violin with three strings that can be played with a bow or plucked. Perhaps the Captain is one of the other spirits still playing and enjoying the unique sounds of this instrument.

Protective Ghost of Drowned Keeper

Penfield Reef Light, Fairfield, Connecticut

Penfield Reef is a hazardous landmass situated about a mile off the coast of Fairfield, near Bridgeport, Connecticut, in Long Island Sound. In 1864, while transporting passengers, the steamer *Rip Van Winkle* ran aground on the reef, though no injuries were reported. Most mariners recognized the reef as one of the most perilous ledges in the region. After numerous shipwrecks near the rocks, a lighthouse was built in 1874. It is said to be haunted by the ghost of a former keeper who drowned and now helps mariners in stormy weather.

Storm clouds dispersing at Penfield Reef Light

In 1916, a series of fierce storms in the region began in early November. Just before Thanksgiving on November 23, one of these devastating storms caught ten barges carrying pig iron, coal, and sand under tow by the giant tugboat *John Garret*. As they approached Penfield Reef, the winds had intensified to gale force when the tow suddenly parted in the middle, sending the barges floundering in the churning waters. A barge named *Grandma* broke in two almost immediately, while the barge *Dorothy* capsized as the high winds and waves maintained their ferocity. Seven other barges began to sink almost in succession. Only one barge, the *Louis*, remained afloat as the crews from all other vessels abandoned their ships in small lifeboats, battling the seas to reach either the tugboat or the surviving barge for safety. Twenty men fought for their lives while the crew members on board the surviving vessels assisted in their rescue. Fortunately, all were saved and brought to Bridgeport.

Keeper Frederick Jordan had not seen his family for weeks due to the storms. He had to tend to the lighthouse day and night with little sleep until Assistant Keeper Rudolph Iten could finally leave the shore during a lull in the weather to relieve him. On a cold Friday morning, December 22, 1916, it seemed the storms had subsided, and the keeper decided this would be a perfect opportunity to go ashore and spend the holiday with his family. He planned to row to Bridgeport and catch a steamship to his home in Port Jefferson, located on the Long Island shore in nearby New York, where his wife and two children awaited him. He remained unaware of the gale-force winds approaching Long Island Sound and the Connecticut shoreline, churning the waters.

Jordan placed the handmade wooden Christmas presents he had crafted at the lighthouse into a dory and set out around 1:30 p.m. that afternoon as the winds and waves intensified. Determined to see his family, the keeper rowed toward the shore while Assistant Keeper Iten watched from the lighthouse. Jordan was a few hundred yards from the beacon when the winds gusted to gale force, and heaving waves tossed his boat about. Suddenly, a large sea swell produced a massive wave that swept over the craft, throwing the keeper into the icy water.

Iten watched in horror as his friend struggled in the white-capped waters. Grabbing the other dory, he tried to row toward Keeper Jordan, but the shifting winds and outgoing tides worked against him. He couldn't bring his boat anywhere close to the keeper, who had drifted nearly half a mile away from the lighthouse, clinging to the craft for dear life and crying for help. Fearing for his own safety, Iten had to abandon the rescue and watch Jordan drift helplessly away, ultimately drowning in the frigid sea. Iten himself barely escaped the same fate as the seas pitched his boat around effortlessly. He struggled against the storm with all his might and was able to return to the lighthouse's rocky shore as waves were breaking all around.

Communication from the lighthouse was down for several days. On Tuesday, December 26, a tugboat was dispatched, carrying the Bridgeport harbor master and a lighthouse keeper from New York to ensure everything was alright at Penfield Reef Lighthouse as the storm raged on. The tug could only get close enough to the reef for Iten and the harbor master to communicate using megaphones. The assistant relayed what had happened to Keeper Jordan while the tug struggled against the dangerously high waves. After receiving the tragic news, the tug returned to shore. Upon learning of the keeper's death, Sheriff William H. Gould enlisted more than a hundred men to search the Connecticut shore for Keeper Jordan's body, but they were unable to find it.

Iten remained as an interim keeper until an inquiry had cleared him of any wrongdoing in the incident, as he had tried to save the keeper and then had to save his own life in that devastating storm. He was close to the keeper and felt he had also lost a good friend. He was promoted to the keeper position at Penfield Reef Light and was provided an assistant named Charles Reuter to aid him with his duties. Over the next few weeks, Iten claimed he felt a constant, unearthly chill in the lighthouse and observed a hazy presence emerging from the deceased keeper's former room.

A few months later, on March 12, 1917, the body of a man washed ashore across the sound near the village of Riverhead, New York. It was identified as the 38-year-old keeper, Frederick Jordan, on March 22, 1917. At that time, Jordan's family happened to be staying with relatives who lived near the location where he was found, making the discovery a strange coincidence.

A note found on Jordan's body was addressed to Iten, reminding him to complete the log entry in the journal, on the day the keeper had left on December 22. A few days later, as a heavy storm approached the region, Iten was working at the desk in the lighthouse when he saw an apparition come down the tower stairs and then vanish. He jumped up to follow but found nothing. When he returned to his desk, he discovered the logbook on the floor, opened to the entry of the day Jordan perished, December 22. Believing it might have been the keeper's spirit, Iten felt compelled to complete the log.

In the following months, Iten reported seeing a hazy figure emerge from the lantern room at various times, noting that the light would behave strangely whenever the apparition appeared. His assistant and others who visited the beacon also saw these unusual events. However, many on the mainland did not believe the keeper's claims, even though all who were witnesses were willing to sign an affidavit to verify what they had observed at the lighthouse. Iten left Penfield Reef Light in 1919, possibly out of despair, allowing his assistant Charles Reuter to take over as keeper until 1920. He then returned as keeper in 1920 and served until his retirement in 1926.

Years later, another keeper at Penfield Reef Light reported seeing the figure of a man dressed entirely in white floating down the tower stairs before vanishing after exiting through the tower door. On stormy and foggy nights, other keepers have observed a ghostly or shadowy figure in the lantern room.

In 1942, a group of boys were fishing near the lighthouse when their boat capsized. A man appeared from the nearby rocky shore, guided the boys to safety at the base of the lighthouse, and then vanished. When they went to thank him at the lighthouse, the current keeper did not recognize whom they were speaking about. After seeing Keeper Jordan's photograph on the wall, the boys identified him as their rescuer.

Decades after Jordan's death, other keepers at the Penfield Reef Lighthouse reported that the light occasionally behaved strangely, particularly just before a storm. To this day, mariners along the Connecticut coast claim to see a human figure on the lantern room gallery or hovering above the reef itself during inclement weather. Many still believe that the ghost of Keeper Jordan watches over the safety of mariners who venture too close to the treacherous reef.

Penfield Reef Light is still haunted by Keeper Jordan protecting mariners.

Bells and Suicidal Assistant Keeper

Stratford Shoal (Middleground) Light, Stratford, Connecticut

The Long Island Sound waterway, located along the borders of New York and Connecticut, features one of the most treacherous channels on the eastern seaboard. With numerous islands, shoals, and reefs, lighthouses were built to help mariners and shipping traffic avoid collisions with these rocky formations during stormy weather. Stratford Shoal Lighthouse, also known as "Middleground" light, is situated on a rocky shoal approximately a mile in diameter, most of which is submerged about nine feet below sea level.

The lighthouse stands halfway between Stratford Point in Connecticut and Old Field Point on Long Island, New York. Although it was originally scheduled for completion around 1872, persistent severe weather postponed its completion until 1878. Its architectural design included a 60-foot granite tower built to withstand harsh weather conditions. However, due to its distance from either shore exceeding five miles, it became an isolated and undesirable location for many of the lighthouse keepers assigned there. Two paranormal events have led mariners to consider this beacon the most haunted in Connecticut.

Stratford Shoal (Middleground) Light after storm breaks up.

Church Bells Under the Sea

In the early 1800s, before the lighthouse was constructed, the ship *Trustful* was preparing to set sail from Bridgeport with a cargo of church bells as a major storm approached. As the seas began to swell, some crew members started discussing the possibility of staying on land and abandoning the ship. The captain, alerted to the situation, warned all crew members that the "bells would toll a dirge for the white-livered folk" who stayed behind if the ship sank. Reluctantly, the crew chose to remain aboard, and, almost as if it were a prophecy, the vessel ran aground on Stratford Shoal and sank, drowning everyone on board. Many mariners have since claimed that when approaching the shoal in foul weather, the muffled sound of church bells can be heard beneath the waves.

The Suicidal Assistant Keeper

Gilburt Rulon served as the keeper of Stratford Shoal Light from 1901 to 1910. Morrell Hulse from Long Island joined the station in 1905 as the first assistant keeper after spending two years in the same role at Whale Rock Light in Rhode Island. That lighthouse was later destroyed in the hurricane of 1938. A young former sailor named Julius Koster, from New York City, arrived at the station in 1904 as the second assistant keeper, marking his first assignment at a lighthouse. The station's remote location posed significant challenges for all three individuals, and Koster began to exhibit signs of depression and anxiety. He also struggled with authority, especially concerning the older 54-year-old Morrell Hulse.

In August 1905, Keeper Rulon went ashore for a well-deserved vacation, leaving his two assistants to manage the light. Koster had just returned from a short shore leave and had consumed three quarts of whiskey. The two men got into an argument, during which Koster produced a razor tied to a pole from a boat hook he had crafted. He charged at Hulse with the improvised weapon, but the aggressor was subdued as the victim managed to calm him down.

In the following days, the two argued and fought as Koster continued his attempts to harm the older assistant keeper. Hulse struggled to get much sleep, worrying about Koster's state of mind and his own well-being. He kept his distance as much as possible and would sneak out to ensure the light was properly maintained and functioning while keeping a watchful eye out.

One afternoon, five days after the keeper had left, Hulse found Koster using a hammer and chisel on the lighthouse wall, attempting to remove the bricks from the tower, stating he was after someone. Hulse managed to convince him to stop causing any further damage. Later that evening, Hulse noticed that the light had stopped rotating. He hurried to the lantern room and discovered Koster armed with an axe driving spikes in the machinery, ready to smash the lens. Hulse rushed in and overpowered the assailant once more.

The following day, Koster, feeling calmer but in a more depressive state, repeatedly threatened to take his own life, prompting Hulse to keep engaging in active conversations with him. When Keeper Rulon returned the next day from vacation, he and Hulse found that Koster had already inflicted wounds on his neck. He was discharged from service and transported to a New York sanitarium for evaluation. Some reports suggest he committed suicide shortly after arriving, while others indicate he was released back to New York City, where he ultimately took his own life.

Although Julius Koster did not die at the lighthouse, many believe his spirit haunts the area. Keepers and Coast Guardsmen have reported doors slamming in the middle of the night, chairs being thrown against the walls, and posters being ripped down. Hot water pans while caretakers were cooking have also been witnessed flying off the stove and crashing onto the floor.

Stratford Shoal (Middleground) Light haunted by suicidal assistant keeper.

Ghost of "Ernie," and Others

New London Ledge Light, New London, Connecticut

Before New London Ledge Lighthouse was built in 1909, ships entering the area had to carefully navigate around a dangerous ledge about a mile from the shore, which marked the entrance to New London Harbor. The lighthouse, constructed on this ledge, showcases an elegant brick design. This distinctive structure was built in response to requests from wealthy locals for an ornate building to complement their upscale coastal community homes.

New London Ledge Light lies about a mile offshore.

New London Ledge Light is one of New England's most renowned haunted lighthouses. The ghost known as "Ernie" has reportedly been heard by many keepers and Coast Guardsmen who have maintained the beacon. Numerous stories attempt to identify who "Ernie" was, with credible accounts from many respected individuals who served at the lighthouse for years, claiming to have heard and witnessed strange noises and events at this location. There is also a belief that more than one spirit may inhabit the lighthouse. Additionally, there were reports of unusual occurrences during the lighthouse construction in the early 1900s, such as the disappearance and reappearance of equipment.

Throughout much of the lighthouse's history, those who tended it, including keepers and Coast Guardsmen, often blamed "Ernie" for the eerie occurrences surrounding the facility. Tools would mysteriously disappear only to reappear; items would be rearranged, floors would unexpectedly be washed, brass would be polished, windows cleaned, and more. One keeper recounted finding open paint cans with brushes, witnessing cups sliding across tables, and doors opening and closing on their own. There were also issues with a TV that would turn on and off, and the foghorn would sound unexpectedly without explanation. Boats belonging to local mariners and tourists tied to the shore mysteriously drifted away. One time, some fishermen who stopped by the lighthouse for coffee expressed skepticism about the ghost's existence. However, when it was time to leave, they discovered their boat had been set adrift.

Keeper's Lost Love

The most widely told story involves a keeper who lost his wife to a ferry captain. Life as a lighthouse keeper was challenging and often lonely. If a keeper brought his wife along, it could become even more difficult for her due to the limited social interaction and isolation it presented. This may have been the situation at New London Ledge Lighthouse in the early 1930s, where it is said that a newlywed keeper had a much younger wife who craved the company of others. She earned a reputation as quite the flirt among local fishermen and sailors passing by the lighthouse. One day, when the keeper went ashore to gather necessary supplies, she left a note stating that she had run away with the Block Island Ferry captain and was never seen again. When the keeper discovered that his new bride would never return, he was overwhelmed with despair. Legend has it that he slit his throat with a fishing knife at the top of the lighthouse tower and fell 65 feet to his death on the rocks below. However, there is no record of any suicide attempt.

The story above draws from findings reported in December 1981, when Dr. Roger Pile, a "ghost psychologist," visited the lighthouse with his wife, who claimed to be a medium. According to the Piles, the spirit they encountered was a keeper named John Randolph, who was not married but had lost his beloved sweetheart due to their terrible argument. However, there is no record of a keeper named John Randolph. The lighthouse station also housed only single men at that time, so if this version has any truth, it would pertain to a girlfriend someone had intended to marry. There were also rumors that John Randolph's middle name was Ernie, which may provide explanation to the ghost's nickname.

The Lady of the Ledge

Another story may shed light on some of the frequent hauntings involving another spirit alongside Ernie. Around 1914, a couple and their daughter departed from New Jersey for New Bedford, Massachusetts, aboard their sailboat and found themselves caught in a terrible storm. That night, the keeper spotted the couple frantically swimming toward the lighthouse and hurried out to assist them in reaching the shore safely. They informed him that their boat had capsized in the storm and they couldn't locate their daughter. After promising to help them find her, he provided them with warm clothing so that the couple could sleep in a spare room that night.

He woke up early the next day to find that the pair had vanished without a trace. A few days later, the keeper went to shore for supplies when the seas had calmed. Some workers on the shore told him they had rescued a young woman who claimed her parents were lost in a sailboat wreck. However, like the couple he believed he had saved that night, this woman had also mysteriously disappeared. Over the years, people have encountered the spirit of a middle-aged woman roaming the lighthouse in search of a loved one, and she has been named "The Lady of the Ledge."

A New Twist on "Ernie"

The noises, prank events, and visions persisted over the years as the lighthouse remained haunted. New London Ledge Light was automated in 1987. On the last day before automation, a Coast Guardsman entered in the log: "Rock of slow torture. Ernie's domain. Hell on earth -- may New London Ledge's light shine on forever because I'm through. I will watch it from afar while drinking a brew."

In the early 2000s, paranormal investigator Christine Kaczynski and her team were invited to investigate the hauntings at New London Ledge Light multiple times. Her findings suggest that the lighthouse experiences significant spirit activity. She reported that most of this activity takes place on the third floor of the building, specifically in the northeast corner. She also believed there might be more than one spirit present, but assured that they are neither dangerous nor evil.

A few years later, researchers from the New England Ghost Project were invited to investigate. They brought specialized equipment to measure EVPs (electronic voice phenomena), which could record faint auditory disturbances by filtering background noise. Most ghost hunters prefer this equipment because it captures "spiritual voices." The team identified at least two distinctly different voices in their findings, leading to the belief that multiple spirits resided at the lighthouse. They asked one of the spirits, "Are you here?" to which a reply was discernible as "Yes." Another recording from a different room stated, "I am cold." In another area of the lighthouse, a team member asked, "Do you like us here?" An audible response was captured as "Yes."

The researchers contacted an unhappy spirit claiming to be a construction worker who accidentally fell to his death after his coworkers played a prank on him by locking him out on the roof. The spirit communicated with the psychic that the tragic incident had been covered up. This event offered an alternative and more realistic perspective than other "Ernie" stories. This potentially explains the reasoning as to the absence of any written documentation about any lighthouse keeper committing suicide there.

Over the years, invited psychics have attempted to persuade the spirits to leave the beacon. However, their efforts have been unsuccessful. It appears these entities are content to remain at the lighthouse.

New London Ledge Light remains haunted.

Haunted Lighthouses in Rhode Island

Rhode Island, often referred to as the "Ocean State," may be the smallest state in the United States. However, it boasts around 400 miles of densely populated coastline and has its share of perilous reefs, ledges, and sandbars that have challenged mariners for many years. The largest island, Block Island, features two lighthouses, to guide sailors through Block Island Sound. One of these, the Block Island Southeast Light, is rumored to be haunted by an angry female spirit, and there have been sightings of a ghost ship named the *Palatine*, also known as the "Flying Dutchman" near the island shores.

On the mainland, Conanicut Island and Prudence Island, along with many smaller islands, separate Rhode Island's Narragansett Bay into two channels: the East Passage and the West Passage. Due to numerous hazardous ledges, islands, and Rhode Island's rugged coastline, lighthouses were constructed to guide mariners and shipping traffic from Newport to Providence and along the western side towards Connecticut. On the west side, Watch Hill Light is said to be haunted by a young, playful spirit, while spirits from the tragedy of a murder-suicide haunt Conimicut Lighthouse.

The capital city of Newport became a haven for extremely wealthy individuals who amassed their fortunes during the 19th century. Many were involved in the whaling industry, while others took part in the notorious Triangle Trade, where African slaves were exchanged in the West Indies for sugar and molasses, which were then used to produce rum in Newport. At one point, it was estimated that one in four residents of Newport earned their living in some capacity related to the sea. In Newport Harbor, unusual paranormal activity has been reported at Rose Island Light and Fort Hamilton nearby.

Mad Maggie

Block Island Southeast Light, Shoreham, Rhode Island

Block Island is about 12 miles south of the Rhode Island mainland and about the same distance northeast of Montauk Point, New York. This island of seven miles in length was a resort for the wealthy and is still a major player in Rhode Island's tourism industry today. However, for centuries, it was also known by mariners for its hazardous reefs and frequent fog. Two lighthouses were built on Block Island to guide shipping traffic and local fishermen along Block Island Sound entering and leaving the island. Block Island's Southeast Lighthouse, built in 1875, is currently sitting at 200 feet above sea level over a sandy bluff. It is New England's highest beacon, with its tower lantern measuring 258 feet above sea level. Renowned for its Gothic-style architecture, the lighthouse was considered one of the grandest in the nation.

When the lighthouse was originally built, it stood three hundred feet away from the edge of the Mohegan Bluffs and the ocean. Over the next hundred years the bluff eroded to within seventy-five feet of the light. To avoid a catastrophe, funds were raised, and the beacon was finally moved in 1993.

Gothic structure of Block Island Southeast Lighthouse.

A rumored murder victim, the former wife of a lighthouse keeper, is believed to haunt the lighthouse as an angry poltergeist, even after the structure was relocated from the eroding cliffs in 1993. This story begins in the early 1900s, when a keeper had a violent argument with his allegedly nagging wife, who felt bored and depressed in the lighthouse. In a fit of rage, he pushed her down the tower's stairs, which resulted in her death from a broken neck. Their marriage was known to be very contentious among the locals. In defending himself, he claimed that in a moment of anger or despair, she threw herself down the stairs. The authorities quickly relieved him of his duties; he was arrested, charged with murder, convicted, and sent to prison, never to return to the lighthouse. However, no newspaper articles about this event can be found, and there is no evidence of a keeper being removed for killing his wife.

There is, however, evidence of some spirit at the lighthouse based on numerous reports over the years. Many islanders believe that "Mad Maggie," as she is known, continues to haunt the lighthouse, targeting male caretakers and visitors. They report being victims of this poltergeist's wrath, claiming they were locked in rooms and closets, had their beds lifted and shaken, and some insist that sharp objects have been thrown at them. Many have seen her ghost banging or tossing pots and pans, indifferent to whether anyone was watching.

One lone male keeper attempted to sleep one night, but the spirit continued to harass him, banging things and slamming doors. He eventually had enough and dashed outside in his night clothes to chase it, only to discover that the door to the lighthouse had been locked from the inside when he tried to return. The embarrassed keeper managed to enter another building nearby and had to call the Coast Guard to unlock the lighthouse door so he could get back inside. He left the station shortly thereafter.

In 1993, after approximately ten years of fundraising, the lighthouse was relocated about 300 feet back away from the dangerous bluffs. Although many spirits tend to leave when major changes occur, Maggie remains. Since the move, Coast Guardsmen have reported hearing footsteps moving up and down the tower stairs, furniture being rearranged, and food being tossed in the kitchen, as Maggie seems unhappy with the new location. However, women and children who have entered the building have reported no disturbances from this supposed vengeful spirit.

The Palatine Ghost Ship

Block Island, Rhode island

Dangerous sandy shoals and rocky ledges surround Block Island. Dozens of ships perished before the lighthouse authorities decided to construct two distinct lighthouses on either end of the island, Block Island North Light in 1829 and Block Island Southeast Light in 1875. Before the construction of the lighthouses, one of the most famous shipwrecks involved the vessel *Princess Augusta*. It became one of America's renowned phantom ghost ships. The tale resembles the globally recognized legend of the ghost ship *Flying Dutchman* from modern folklore, in which the ship appears to be on fire or translucent from a distance before disappearing.

The *Flying Dutchman,* original color painting by Charles Temple Dix (1860).

The *Princess Augusta* was a Dutch immigrant ship transporting 240 immigrants from Rotterdam in the Netherlands in 1738 to the English colonies in Virginia and Pennsylvania. These settlements were established by many of their fellow countrymen who had come searching for a better life. The passengers hailed from the Palatine region of southwestern Germany, so the ship was called the "*Palatine* ship." After weeks of sailing across the Atlantic through numerous storms and running low on provisions, tensions rose as the ship's water supply became contaminated.

About 200 passengers and half of the 14-member crew succumbed to disease, including the captain. The survivors faced starvation and poor health due to constant exposure to storms. Most of these passengers were poor immigrants with little money. When First Mate Andrew Brook took command, food supplies were running low, and he began charging passengers for their share of the rations. Some starved to death when they ran out of money or items to trade, and they were tossed overboard. Meanwhile, the raging seas pushed the ship off course, causing it to head northwest.

The *Princess Augusta* continued to encounter severe storms off Rhode Island. The ship was constantly battered by waves crashing over its deck as Brook attempted to navigate the vessel between Block Island and Long Island Sound. However, a blinding snowstorm with gale-force winds forced the ship to run aground near the northern tip of Block Island, known as Sandy Point, on December 27, 1738. During a break in the storm, Brook selfishly took only the remaining crew members in the lifeboats and rowed ashore, leaving the immigrant passengers aboard to fend for themselves as best as they could.

At this point, there are different versions of the story. During this period, the residents of Block Island were mainly poor fishermen, regarded as a lower class in 18th century society. Wrecking refers to retrieving cargo from a shipwreck, and coastal inhabitants living where many ships sank were known as wreckers or looters. Many mainlanders believed the islanders to be ruthless characters who plundered and murdered their victims, often fabricating tales of such atrocities. Given that numerous ships were caught in storms off Block Island due to its location along busy shipping lanes, these fishermen were thought to have been directly involved in the practice of looting these doomed vessels.

Block Island beach in northern section.

Block Islanders prefer the story of the residents helping the passengers and crew when the *Princess Augusta,* or *Palatine* ship, wrecked off the island's northern tip. In the islander version, the residents did everything they could to assist, persuading First Mate Brook to let them help retrieve the surviving passengers from the ship the following day and to collect their belongings. They also buried about 20 individuals who died after the wreck. Additionally, they believed that those who survived traveled to the mainland to continue their journey, while some survivors remained on the island.

One of the passengers who stayed on the island, Dutch Kattern, was notorious as a known witch and may have fueled some of the stories, as she exhibited odd behavior around the anniversary of the incident and was seen trying to cast spells to summon the ghost ship. Reports suggest that the ship was considered not salvageable and was pushed out to sea to sink. Depositions, written at the time for the creditors of the wreck, reveal that the surviving crew members faced no charges for their actions. It was believed that they, along with most of the surviving passengers, reached the mainland, after which little is known about them, deepening the mystery of what actually occurred.

The other, a more horrific version told by mainlanders and many mariners, became more widely adopted after the famous poet John Greenleaf Whittier wrote "The Palatine" in 1867. He fueled the notion that the residents lured the ship onto Block Island with a false signal light, causing it to wreck offshore. Although the islanders allowed the surviving passengers and crew to land, they plundered the ship. The vessel was completely stripped, and the locals chose to burn the boat's remains to clear the way for other ships or to destroy any evidence of crimes committed. Once they had taken all they could carry, the looters set fire to the vessel and let it drift out to sea with the tide.

In most versions, the islanders and survivors were unaware that one frightened immigrant, Mary Vanderline (or Van Der Line), had remained on board. However, some accounts suggest she outright refused to abandon the ship. Driven mad by the indignities of the entire ordeal, she did not want to leave whatever remained of her possessions and was too terrified to come ashore. The ship drifted out to sea, engulfed in flames, and unconfirmed reports say that local mariners could hear the screams of the unfortunate immigrant that night as the blazing vessel vanished beneath the waves.

A year later, the islanders would write about observing the "Palatine Light" a few miles offshore as a burning ship. This phenomenon would be seen again in early winter and recorded by islanders, mariners, and tourists alike for many years afterward, and it remains unexplained to this day. Those who were more religious and observed the phenomenon shortly after the ship's burning believed it to be a warning from an "Almighty Power."

Today, the *Palatine* has become one of America's most famous phantom ghost ships and has evolved into folklore as "The Flying Dutchman," often seen sailing off the coast of Block Island in early winter, frequently appearing in flames. Written accounts from Block Island residents describe a flickering light visible from a distance, miles away from the northern part of the island, resembling a giant torch and typically sailing parallel to the shore or sometimes appearing as a small light where no other ships were in sight.

An islander named Dr. Aaron C. Willey described the light decades later in 1811 after claiming to have seen it several times himself. Nearly 200 years later, members of the Block Island Historical Society placed a marker at the site where twenty passengers were buried. No remains of the wreck have ever been found.

Huge sandy bluffs over beach on Block Island.

Playful Young Spirit

Watch Hill Light, Westerly, Rhode Island

Watch Hill got its name during King George's War, in the 1740's when a watchtower was built to warn residents against naval attacks. The tower proved helpful in the 1750s during the French and Indian Wars, where daily smoke signals and nightly bonfires from the tower helped to warn local fishermen and merchant ships when French pirates were in the area.

With the number of recorded shipwrecks on the treacherous rocky shoals around Watch Hill rising, residents petitioned to construct a lighthouse. President Thomas Jefferson ordered the lighthouse's construction, which was completed in 1808. Watch Hill Lighthouse is the second oldest beacon in Rhode Island. It is believed to be haunted by a young spirit.

Watch Hill Lighthouse at low tide.

One story centers on the death of a small child, possibly the offspring of a Coast Guardsman or a staff member who was assigned to the lighthouse many years ago. The edge of the small peninsula where the lighthouse stands frequently erodes and can be very dangerous, as rocks now encircle the seawall. Apparently, the child was playing on the rocks, as children often do, and fell, leading to his death from the injuries sustained.

One of the last Coast Guard families stationed at the lighthouse before its automation had encounters with whom they believed to be the spirit of a young child. They participated in the local scout troop with their two boys. The family was very close-knit and enjoyed living and working at the lighthouse. They hosted numerous events and camp outs there, fostering a strong sense of community participation.

The keeper's house had the creaks and noises typical of an old structure facing the sea. During their stay, however, the couple experienced the footsteps and laughter of a young ghost. They remained very relaxed and were not bothered by it, keeping most of these encounters to themselves, as they never felt threatened. They believed him to be a small boy, possibly 8 to 10 years old. He was occasionally a little unsettling but never frightening. The keeper conducted some informal inquiries and discovered that a caretaker may have lost a child there many years ago.

One incident occurred when the keeper's wife was home one day after school. The boys played a reasonable distance from the house while she did chores and prepared supper. Suddenly, the door opened, and someone quickly entered the kitchen, darting behind her before running into another room as she faced the window by the sink. She caught a glimpse of him from the corner of her eye and called after him to slow down and be careful, but there was no response. Looking out the window, she noticed that both her sons were still playing outside. Whoever had rushed past her wasn't one of her children.

On another occasion, the keeper was sitting in the kitchen late at night when someone approached him from behind and said, "Dad" or "Daddy." He turned around, but no one was there. He checked on his family, and everyone was either upstairs or had already gone to sleep. Neither he nor his wife felt frightened or uneasy about these encounters.

Some of these sightings were reported many years ago, and there have been accounts of a female spirit in the house, believed to possibly be the mother. Given the numerous shipwrecks near the lighthouse over the years, the spirit(s) may have originated from one of these wrecks. No incidents have been reported for years, as no families currently reside there. Perhaps the young child spirit felt most comfortable when loving families occupied the lighthouse.

Murder-Suicide by Distraught Wife

Conimicut Shoal Light, Warwick, Rhode Island

Conimicut Shoal Lighthouse is located at the Providence River entrance in Narragansett Bay, perched on Conimicut Point Shoal. Built in 1868, early keepers were not given living quarters at the lighthouse and had to make daily mile-long trips, sometimes quite perilous, in a rowboat to the nearby Nayatt Point Lighthouse on shore for overnight stays. Years later, in 1873, a five-room keeper's dwelling was constructed on the landing pier connected to the tower. The current tower is haunted resulting from a tragic murder-suicide.

Conimicut Shoal Lighthouse hauntings from murder-suicide.

Ellsworth J. Smith was first appointed keeper of Great Beds Lighthouse in New Jersey in 1916. The beacon stood less than a mile from the busy shore, allowing the keeper to easily escape the confines of the tower. He was a lonely 40-year-old man who decided to advertise for a new bride in hopes of starting a family at the lighthouse. After three months of advertising, Helen Barry from New Haven, Connecticut, responded to his ad. However, upon her arrival in Perth Amboy, New Jersey, the city clerk refused to issue the couple a wedding license because Helen disclosed that she was only sixteen. The issue was resolved, as a newspaper article reported months later that Smith's young bride from New Haven, Connecticut, had been residing at Great Beds Lighthouse for several weeks. Presumably, the couple traveled to Connecticut, where the minimum age for marriage was less strict, to obtain a legal wedding license.

Helen was known by the nickname Nellie, which was quite popular at that time. In 1922, Ellsworth J. Smith took over as the keeper of Conimicut Shoal Lighthouse. By then, the couple had been married for six years and had two children: a two-year-old named Russel and his older brother, Robert, who was five. The lighthouse was located in a more remote and rural area than Great Beds Light, providing fewer opportunities for social activities. Keeper Ellsworth wanted the entire family to live at the lighthouse and work together as a family unit. However, this daily routine of maintaining the lighthouse and its buildings did not sit well with the young mother, who longed to socialize with women her age on the mainland.

As the weeks went by, Nellie constantly begged her husband to let her go ashore, but he repeatedly reminded her of her duties at the lighthouse. She grew increasingly depressed and implored him to allow her to leave, even threatening to take her own life multiple times if he didn't grant her request. Smith continued to decline her pleas, perhaps due to jealousy stemming from her significantly younger age. Nellie came to realize that the isolation at the lighthouse was unbearable and began contemplating a way to end her life and that of her children.

In the days before antibiotics, physicians used mercury chloride to treat various diseases, especially syphilis. It was also given in a very diluted form for tonsillitis and other ailments. However, just three tablets can be lethal to an adult, and in the early 20th century, most people could buy them at a pharmacy without a prescription. Keeper Smith kept some of these pills in a medicine cabinet at the lighthouse.

On June 9, 1922, around 10 a.m., Keeper Smith left for Conimicut Village to get supplies while Nellie played with the children. When she noticed the keeper was out of sight, she opened the medicine cabinet and took out some mercury chloride tablets. Nellie told five-year-old Robert that she was going to put his little brother to bed. She placed two-year-old Russell on her lap and gave him a tablet, which the toddler willingly took. She told Robert she would also give him some candy when she returned downstairs to join him. She took the toddler upstairs to his bedroom and laid him on his bed, where he soon fell back unconscious.

In tears, she returned downstairs and sat at the table with Robert. She gave him a couple of the tablets, while she took a few for herself and laid her head down on the table near him. The young boy couldn't handle the bitter taste, and after trying to swallow the pills unsuccessfully, he spat them out as he watched his mother slump onto the table into unconsciousness, thinking she was in a deep sleep. Meanwhile, he began to feel stomach pains.

It was 4 p.m., when Keeper Smith returned to Conimicut Shoal Lighthouse with a boat full of supplies. He called out for assistance with the load, but no one answered. He entered the house with two armloads of groceries into the kitchen and found his wife and Robert at the table. Robert was pale and looking too sick to talk. He called out to Nellie but didn't get any response. He put down the bags and shook her shoulder, then lifted her arm above her head, let it go, and watched it drop without resistance. He knew she was dead. Looking around the house for Russell, he finally ran upstairs to the bedroom and found the toddler in his bed; he had perished.

In a state of shock and grief, the keeper rushed downstairs to retrieve Robert, who was groaning and suffering from the effects of the poison he had spat out. He quickly placed his son in the dory and rowed the mile-long journey back to shore to find the doctor's office for help. When they arrived the young boy was doubled over in pain. After the doctor and his staff administered an antidote and conducted careful routine observations, Robert slowly recovered from the ordeal. Once the boy was stable enough to be moved, he was taken to the home of his aunt, where he could be closely monitored. Smith then had to attend to making funeral arrangements and other responsibilities in the aftermath of such a tragedy.

Keeper Smith, always responsible for the lighthouse, notified the proper authorities that he had to abandon the lighthouse as the beacon remained dark that night, prompting a warning to mariners and those on shore nearby. He would tell the authorities and reporters that his wife had repeatedly urged him to give up his post at the lighthouse, which he said he promised to do before the following winter. In the newspapers, Nellie's age is given as thirty, which the keeper likely reported deliberately to avoid public scrutiny regarding her younger age and to grant her peace. Nellie and Russell were quietly buried in a grave near East Greenwich, Rhode Island. Unable to return to the lighthouse daily and relive the incident, Keeper Ellsworth J. Smith retired.

Since the tragedies, future keepers and Coast Guard personnel have reported strange occurrences at the lighthouse. Some have reported to have heard a woman crying and a young child laughing when no one else was present. Some of reported observing a sad-faced woman descending down the stairs and then disappearing into the kitchen. Others have mentioned that items and tools have been moved from their original locations.

Post card (circa 1907).
Rhode Island News Company

A few years ago, I interviewed former lighthouse keeper Paul Baptiste for a book on famous shipwrecks and rescues around New England lighthouses, and I wanted to share his story. He served at Bakers Island Light in Massachusetts and at Monhegan Island Light in Maine. Paul, in his eighties, was one of the last keepers around from the 1940s and 1950s, and had retired in 1962. Paul recounted that in 1950, Keeper Nelson H. Powell of Conimicut Shoal Light needed to return to shore for a few days, and Paul, stationed at Bakers Island Light, was obliged to help tend the light in his absence. The grateful keeper left his wife behind, and Paul stayed in one of the rooms beneath the lantern room.

That first night, he slept soundly and spent the day tending to the light. On the second night, Powell's wife asked if he had seen the ghost of Mrs. Smith. She explained that a former keeper's wife had murdered her youngest son in the same room where Paul was sleeping, then took her own life. She also claimed to have seen the ghost of the mother. This revelation frightened him so much that he stayed awake all night. Although he never encountered any ghosts, he felt relieved when Keeper Powell returned the next day. Paul never went back to Conimicut Shoal Light again.

Keeper Curtis & Quarantine Victims

Rose Island Light, Newport, Rhode Island

During the Revolutionary War, both the British and the Colonists utilized Rose Island to defend Newport. After the Revolution, in 1794, Congress authorized the construction of fortifications at strategic harbors, including Narragansett Bay, as part of the American Seacoast Defense System. French engineers were commissioned to build the largest fort, Fort Hamilton, which was only partially completed. For decades, military construction on the island remained minimal. However, the fort barracks functioned as a quarantine station for cholera victims in the 1820s and for individuals afflicted with yellow fever in the 1850s. With so many souls that had perished within these walls, numerous paranormal events have been witnessed over the years.

After the Civil War ended in 1865, Rhode Island experienced an increase in shipping traffic and tourism connecting Newport, Boston, and New York. The construction of the Rose Island Lighthouse, located about a mile from the Newport shore, began in 1869 and was completed in 1870. In 1883, the island started building additional structures for storing explosives. These storage facilities were later used during World War II to hold torpedoes manufactured by the Goat Island factory nearby. Charles Curtis became the keeper a few years later, in 1887. He remained dedicated to the lighthouse for 31 years; however, it is said that his ghost still visits and tends to the beacon.

Rose Island Lighthouse as fog begins to lift with bridge in background.

Aerial view Rose Island Lighthouse and Fort Hamilton barracks on right side.
Image Library of Congress

Souls of Quarantine Victims

In the nineteenth century, quarantine stations were established on islands to isolate those infected with contagious diseases from mainland populations. Rose Island, already home to Fort Hamilton barracks with 3-foot and 4-foot-thick stone walls designed to withstand explosions and protect hundreds of soldiers, served as the local quarantine station throughout the 1800s. The small island contains two mass graves, as noted in logbook entries by previous lighthouse keepers; however, their exact locations remain a mystery as they are unmarked. The barracks and lighthouse are thought to be haunted by the spirits of those who died of illnesses there. Reports have emerged of footsteps, slamming doors, and other noises around these structures, along with sightings of ghostly images wandering the grounds..

During the hurricane of 1938, massive tidal surges swept over and around the island, uncovering some of the bodies that had been buried. Witnesses reported that the clothing appeared to be from the Civil War period. Later, while workers were excavating an area of the island to build a water tower, they unearthed skeletons also dressed in Civil War-era clothing. The remains were promptly reburied on the island. Some believe these events may have sparked reported sightings and noises since the spirits of these souls might have become restless. Recently, an overnight visitor at the lighthouse claimed that something was typing on her iPad, and the keys lit up as it typed, "I am Ena. I live here."

Keeper Charles Curtis Still Tends the Lighthouse

Charles S. Curtis was a Civil War veteran who became the keeper of Rose Island Light in 1887. His 31-year tenure (1887-1918) is the longest in Rhode Island's history for a keeper tending the same beacon. Keeper Curtis loved the island and lighthouse, took his duties seriously, and raised his family there. Charles and his wife, Christina, had a daughter named Mabel, whose child, Wanton, was a sickly baby. They helped raise him in the salt-fresh air at the lighthouse until he was able to attend school. Apparently, it served him well, as it was discovered many years later during a CT scan that his heart was on the other side of his chest and he had only one lung, but he lived to the age of 99!

On April 21, 1894, Keeper Curtis's son witnessed two grave robbers exhuming two bodies from graves on the island. He sought help and started to pursue the men, but they escaped in a boat and vanished into the fog.

During the first two weeks of February 1899, the region experienced some of the coldest winter weather in its history. Temperatures dropped below zero for over a week, and a blizzard struck Newport on February 10, lasting several days. Parts of Newport Harbor froze during the storm, trapping Keeper Curtis and his family on Rose Island so they could not get food supplies or coal to heat the lighthouse. Some family members fell ill and required assistance. On February 14, Curtis turned the American flag upside down and hoisted it on the flagpole as a distress signal. Officers of the Revenue Cutter *Dexter* noticed the signal and rushed to his aid. The vessel had to break through dangerous ice flows to reach Rose Island Lighthouse. They transported the sick family members to the nearby Goat Island torpedo station for medical attention and brought back food and coal to the lighthouse.

Keeper Curtis earned two life-saving medals during his tenure. One of these was awarded in 1914, when he was recognized for rescuing men from a disabled powerboat that was swiftly heading out to sea. He was 73 years old at the time of this rescue.

Congress passed a bill in 1918 mandating that all officers and employees of the Lighthouse Service reaching the age of seventy had to retire. As Keeper Charles Curtis approached his 79th birthday, he was forced to retire at the end of 1918, but he did receive the maximum possible retirement benefits. The keeper died a few years later, in 1922.

Many reports suggest that his spirit still roams the lighthouse, ensuring everything is in order. In his life, his daily routine included a 12-hour shift that ended at midnight. Each night, Keeper Curtis would descend the tower stairs from the lantern room and head to the kitchen for a glass of milk. After his death, visitors and staff often reported hearing footsteps coming down the stairs, which would typically stop in the kitchen.

Rose Island Lighthouse is the most haunted beacon in Rhode Island.

Various Investigators Validating

Over the years, various teams of paranormal investigators have been invited to Rose Island and the lighthouse to validate the numerous sightings and events reported by staff members and visitors alike. In 2010, the Ghost Hunters TV show team was invited to the island (Season 6, Episode 15). The TAPS team was shown unusual photographs that contained possible orbs of light, and a framed current photograph of Rose Island Lighthouse with a reflection of a face of what appeared as someone in a vintage uniform in the glass. They were informed of accounts of apparitions, footsteps, doors opening and closing, and other strange noises and voices as the crew explored Rose Island. While they were investigating the keeper's quarters, they registered a high reading from the closet, but when the door was opened, the activity ceased, followed by a child-like voice that sounded like a doll saying "Mama." Murmuring noises were also heard in the lantern room with no explanation.

Outside the barracks by the fort, other members observed a "white mass" or some type of light anomaly in one of the camera feeds that could not be explained. While investigating the light source, they heard a door open and faint voices in the fort's quarantine room. In their reveal, in regards to the mysterious photo displaying a reflection of a vintage face in the glass, they verified that the image strongly resembled the keeper, Charles Curtis.

Dave McCurty served as the director of the Rose Island Lighthouse Foundation. He and his wife had been hearing doors slam and other noises emanating from the second floor of the lighthouse. They invited a group of investigators from the New England Ghost Project, led by Ron Kolek, to examine the lighthouse. On the night of the investigation, three investigators sat in complete darkness downstairs. The lead investigator asked, "Are you willing to try some table tipping?" The other two, who were not sure of what he was talking about, agreed and gathered around a small end table, where they were advised to place their fingertips on the table surface. He then urged the spirits to move the table as a sign of their presence, provided they meant no harm. Suddenly, the table started to move and wobble in front of the startled men.

Around 2 a.m. that same night, the three who had witnessed the table wobbling downstairs joined five others upstairs to contact spirits around a large oak table. Most members felt it was too big and heavy to be moved, but six sat around it and decided to give it a try. Once again, the head investigator had the team members place their fingertips on the table's surface and asked the spirits to make themselves known, provided they meant no harm. The table began to vibrate and then started to rock and jump off the floor, much to the crew's excitement. In fact, the table lifted slightly a couple of inches for a few seconds, to the amazement of the team members.

The entities that inhabit the lighthouse and nearby barracks of Fort Hamilton appear peaceful, if not playful, as verified by the various teams of investigators invited to validate their existence. Keeper Curtis appears to enjoy the company of the caretakers and takes pride in ensuring that the lighthouse remains in as good condition as he left it many years ago.

Haunted Lighthouses in Massachusetts

Along the Massachusetts coastline, shipping traffic typically followed the same route to avoid being caught in the open sea during fast-approaching storms in New England. This route involved navigating through Vineyard Sound off western Massachusetts, along Buzzards Bay, between the large islands of Martha's Vineyard and Nantucket, and finally along Cape Cod. After rounding Cape Cod, these ships would navigate around the rocky reefs and islands of Boston Harbor or continue to various ports further north along the rugged coastline. With such a high traffic volume, shipwrecks were common, even with the numerous lighthouses built along the coast and on the many islands and shoals. This includes the vast shifting sandbars around Cape Cod that have claimed many lives.

Hauntings vary from possible victims of shipwrecks, or tragic accidents as the "woman in scarlet," on Long Island Head Light, and the rumored murdered wife of the keeper at Bird Island Light. There are sightings of keepers still attending the beacon as those at Minot's Ledge Light, Boston Harbor Light, near Highland Light (Cape Cod) Light, and Gurnet (Plymouth) Light. Some of these are protective spirits like the entities at Borden Flats Light. There are hauntings of heroes in life who remind us of their deeds, as the sisters of Scituate Light, and pranksters that seem to enjoy annoying staff members of Bakers Island Light and nearby cottages in Salem.

Protective, Peaceful, Benign Spirits

Borden Flats Light, Fall River, Massachusetts

The lighthouse, built in 1881, lies on a perilous reef in the middle of the Taunton River, established to accommodate the ever-increasing shipping traffic. Fall River had earned its reputation as the "textile capital of the world." Borden Flats Light was named after the Borden family, a prominent family fixture in the region for generations. However, today, it is better known for the trial of the century, in which daughter Lizzie Borden was accused of murdering her stepmother and father with an axe, but was acquitted. It is still the most famous unsolved murder mystery!

Sunset over the deck of Borden Flats Light.

The house where the incident occurred is near the shore, a short distance from the lighthouse. It is believed to be haunted by the spirits of both victims, her parents, with occurrences including flickering lights, self-opening doors, strange noises, and visions of ghostly figures floating through the rooms. A wooden rocking chair has been seen moving to different locations and then rocking on its own.

Guests who have spent the night in this house, which is currently a bed and breakfast inn and museum that offers ghost tours, have reported hearing children's laughter and the sounds of kids playing, as well as witnessing objects move. These spirits are thought to be the two children of great-aunt Eliza Borden, who, overwhelmed by severe depression, drowned them in the cistern (rainwater barrel) before taking her own life. This tragic event happened decades before the Lizzie Borden case, in the house next door. Talk about having some family issues!

Halfway across the Taunton River from the Lizzie Borden House stands the Borden Flats Lighthouse, which is said to be haunted by two, or possibly three, protective and quiet spirits. One of these spirits is that of the former keeper, John H. Paul, who served from 1912 to 1927 and took part in various rescues. His most notable rescue occurred on August 3, 1912, when he witnessed a rowboat capsizing as two local men attempted to switch places. The keeper rushed to his boat and successfully saved one man from the river's treacherous current, but the other, unable to swim, drowned. For his efforts, John Paul was awarded a bronze Carnegie lifesaving medal for heroism.

After the lighthouse was automated in 1963, and, like many others in those days, it fell into neglect and disrepair. James "Nick" Korstad of Portland, Oregon, purchased it at auction in 2010, with some financial assistance from his parents. Primarily on his own, he spent eight years meticulously restoring and renovating the beacon to its original state of the late 1950s, before it had been automated. He also established a successful overnight light keeper program for visitors to stay overnight.

Offshore station of Borden Flats Lighthouse on the Taunton River.

Since he began restoring Borden Flats Light, Nick noticed he wasn't alone, yet he never felt in danger. While cleaning, he would hear footsteps ascending and descending the tower stairs, which he believed to be the spirit of Keeper John Paul, who still tended to the lighthouse.

The other spirit is that of a 9-year-old girl named Lucy, who tragically drowned when her family's boat capsized near the lighthouse in 1929. Lighthouse Keeper Joe Covo, who was the next keeper after John Paul, sprang into action, rescued her from the waters,

Spiral staircase inside Borden Flats Light.

and brought her back to the lighthouse. He tried desperately to revive her, but unfortunately, she passed away at the lighthouse. She remains a spiritual helper to Keeper John Paul.

To support his belief that friendly spirits were assisting him, Nick invited psychics to the lighthouse to learn about his other guests. The spirit of Keeper John Paul informed the psychics about many of the new keeper's activities there, details they would not have known otherwise. One of the psychics noted that the old keeper recognized Nick as the current keeper but wanted to stay around to ensure he was fulfilling his duties properly.

One day, while cleaning, Nick pleaded with the spirits to keep the seagulls away. Their constant droppings and the littered shells from eating nearby crabs and shellfish were becoming another major clean-up project. The friendly spirits heard him, and to this day, visitors rarely see bird droppings or birds perching on the lighthouse, allowing caretakers to concentrate on maintaining the beacon itself.

The potential third ghost is an unidentified female who has been heard humming. She stays outside of the tower. Nick has reported that John Paul's spirit would not allow her entry inside the caisson tower, but there is no reason given. However, he has heard old classical music playing in the lighthouse and, at times, detected someone scraping paint outside the structure.

As he neared the end of his restoration of the lighthouse, Nick heard less and less of his spiritual guests, as they seemed pleased and preferred not to reveal themselves and stay quiet. In 2018, upon completing his eight-year renovation, he sold the lighthouse to the current owner Kevin Ferias, who continues to provide overnight stays for visitors. Nick used the profits to purchase and restore Big Bay Point Lighthouse on Michigan's Upper Peninsula, currently operating it as a bed and breakfast inn.

Several professional psychics, mediums, and ghost hunters, including the New England Ghost Project and the Southern New England Paranormal group, have been invited to visit the beacon. They have conducted multiple nighttime investigations in the tower and also reported the presence of these quiet, protective, friendly spirits. The experts agreed that they sensed a warm comfort and peace upon entering the lighthouse.

Third floor of Borden Flats Lighthouse, the Entertainment Room.

Since the restoration, only a few rare incidents have occurred in which overnight guests have heard music, footsteps, or laughter during their stays. With the lighthouse fully restored, these friendly spirits are content to remain out of sight and protect their visitors in a very peaceful manner.

On a personal note, my wife and I stayed at the lighthouse on a summer day in August a few years ago and can attest to the wonderful peace that we experienced there. With its interior resembling the late 1950s, it truly is a quiet place to disconnect from the bustling society just half a mile from the shore. We spent the night reading and talking in the third floor "Entertainment Room."

During our stay, few birds, if any, flew directly over the tower. We also noticed no birds perched or left droppings on any part of the lighthouse structure, even while we were eating outdoors, which is unusual. It seems there is some sort of protective barrier or shield over the lighthouse, and it appears that Nick Korstad did receive his wish from the spirits of Keeper John Paul and little Lucy to help keep the lighthouse clean.

Birds rarely fly over Borden Flats Light tower.

Murdered Wife of Keeper?

Bird Island Light, Marion, Massachusetts

Bird Island Lighthouse was built in 1819 on a small rocky island of less than two acres, marking the entrance to Sippican Harbor, which has never had any trees. It was a bustling area frequented by whaling ships and cargo vessels transporting lumber, cut nails, and salt. With pirates lurking in the nearby waters, the tower and the keeper's building were constructed from stone for protection. The island is less than a mile from the mainland.

Bird Island Light about a mile offshore.

The first keeper was William Moore, a veteran of the War of 1812. He was a private, intelligent man who sparked controversy among the townsfolk when he secretly married a young society lady from Boston and brought her to the lighthouse. She was known to have suffered from tuberculosis and had a strong addiction to tobacco, and possibly liquor. There were rumors that he forbade her from socializing onshore and kept her at the lighthouse against her will. Villagers would report that sometimes they heard her cries from the island and visited her, secretly smuggling bags of tobacco and liquor to her in defiance of Keeper Moore's wishes. Some townsfolk also accused Moore of abusing his wife, believing he wouldn't take her ashore for further medical care attention.

When she died a few years later in winter, there was much speculation from the local community that the keeper may have murdered her. Moore buried her in an unmarked grave without any services for the villagers, blaming them for her death by supplying her with tobacco. This further brought stories that maybe he murdered her by shooting her when she was in a drunken stupor dancing in the snow on a cold February morning. Rumors also spread that with the harbor frozen over, Moore raised the distress flag after his wife's death, and a minister walked across the winter ice flows to conduct a simple ceremony for her. Then, he spent several difficult hours with Moore helping to dig her grave in the snow, rocks, and ice-filled dirt.

Keeper Moore left shortly after his wife died in 1822 and was assigned to Billingsgate Lighthouse in the town of Wellfleet on Cape Cod. One story suggests that the keeper who replaced Moore lasted only a couple of weeks, as he left soon after seeing the ghost of a woman outside the keeper's house. Years later, numerous keepers and caretakers reported seeing a ghostly figure of a hunched-over woman knocking at the door of the keeper's house, or a shadowy image of a woman dressed in white lurking in the tower.

Bird Island Light is part of a wildlife sanctuary.

Many years later, when the keeper's dwelling was demolished in 1889, a rifle and a bag of tobacco were discovered in a secret hiding place, further supporting the speculation that her husband had murdered her. However, among those items was a note written by Keeper Moore condemning the villagers. It read:

"This bag contains tobacco, found among the clothes of my wife after her decease. It was furnished by certain individuals in and about Sippican. May the curses of the High Heaven rest upon the heads of those who destroyed the peace of my family and the health and happiness of a wife whom I Dearly Loved."

Spirits Around Cape Cod Light

Highland (Cape Cod) Light, Truro, Massachusetts

The region known as Cape Cod saw a surge in whaling, shipping, and commercial fishing during the 18th and 19th centuries. This increase led to numerous shipwrecks due to its perilous shoals and ever-shifting sandbars. In 1797, Highland Light, also known as Cape Cod Light, was constructed about 500 feet from the edge of a 160-foot bluff, roughly a mile from where many ships had previously sunk in an area of shifting sandy shoals known as the Peaked Hill Bars. Later, to handle the increasingly high volume of maritime traffic, a first-order Fresnel lens, the strongest and most effective type, was installed in 1857. The severity of erosion over many years left the lighthouse with less than 100 feet of space from the edge of the massive cliff. This forced the lighthouse to be moved in 1996 back about 450 feet from its original position.

Highland (Cape Cod) Light near edge of cliffs before being moved back.

Cape Cod is known for numerous sightings of ghosts and other signs of paranormal activity in its houses, inns, taverns, and even an old jail. Over the years, many shipwrecks have happened off its shoals and sandbars in the treacherous waters during foggy and stormy nights, particularly near Highland Lighthouse. The beacon is the oldest lighthouse on the Cape, and many believe it may be haunted by the souls of shipwreck victims and a former keeper. Reports have emerged of footsteps being heard by someone wearing boots leading up to the lantern room, thought to belong to a former lighthouse keeper, although no one knows who it could be. Additionally, unexplained flashing lights near the top of the lighthouse have been seen outside the lantern room. Other mysterious events include sounds of knocking on the door of the keeper's house when no one is present and doors slamming shut.

Much of the paranormal activity centers around structures near the lighthouse. In 1896, a lighthouse keeper (possibly Stephen Rich) and his family reported hearing a ghostly woman's voice in the keeper's house when no one else was present. Following this, additional similar reports emerged. In the 1980s, Coast Guardsman Patrick Prunty heard a woman's voice in the keeper's house while staying with his family.

Storm clouds in the distance of Highland (Cape Cod) Light

Spirits of the Highland House Museum and Jenny Lind Tower

The Highland House Museum is a short distance from Highland Light. The museum showcases several intriguing exhibits on the lower level, many of which are located in the former dining hall of the old hotel. On the second floor there are various rooms with themes reminiscent of the original hotel. The floor includes individual bedrooms for family members, and a general store. Over the years, some guests and former workers have reported seeing a woman dressed in period attire wandering the grounds of the property. There have also been reports of various noises with no one present on the second floor of the hotel.

Recently, some paranormal researchers reported walking up to the second floor and addressed the wandering spirit for signs of its presence. They heard a loud dragging sound coming from an adjacent room. When they rushed into the room, they found that a plastic tarp covering an antique for the winter had moved on its own, creating the scraping sound. Whoever was moving the tarp seemed eager to communicate.

Highland House Museum Circa 1907
Courtesy National Park Service

In 1850, renowned opera singer Jenny Lind, known as the "Swedish Nightingale" was delivering a sold-out performance at the Boston Opera House within the Fitchburg Railroad station, which looked somewhat like a stone castle. Promoter P. T. Barnum oversold the event as a restless crowd gathered outside. The two towers in the front of the station resembled a castle's battlement. Lind reportedly climbed the turret to appease the masses and began singing to her fans below.

In 1927, forty years after the singer's death in 1887, Harry Aldrich, a Boston attorney, purchased the 70-foot tower as the depot was being demolished. He relocated it to his North Truro property just south of Highland Light. In 1932, he brought his family to watch a total eclipse from the top of the tower.

Jenny Lind
Tower

Today, the tower lies between Highland Light and the Truro Air Force Station. Some visitors to the castle-like tower have reported seeing and hearing the spirit of Jenny Lind inside, singing in her melodic voice. Lind's spirit is also associated with folklore regarding the calming of the "Witch of Wellfleet," several miles away, by drowning out the witch's screams that create stormy nights, with her singing.

Hannah Thomas: First Female Keeper

Gurnet Point (Plymouth) Light, Plymouth, Massachusetts

Before the American Revolution began, the area around Plymouth supported a thriving fishing industry and had also become one of the important ports of Colonial America. Other towns nearby were also being recognized as important centers for trade and shipbuilding. Local townsfolk petitioned the Colonial government of Massachusetts for a lighthouse to be built to help guide shipping traffic and mariners through Plymouth Harbor.

John and Hannah Thomas owned a long sandy peninsula at the northern corner of Plymouth Bay. In 1768, the Colonial government requested to have a lighthouse station built on their property, which also marked the entrance to Plymouth Harbor. The agreement allowed John Thomas to be appointed as the first keeper, which was customary in the early days of lighthouse history. This appointment made Thomas one of America's early light keepers in 1769. The lighthouse

Early Twin Towers
of Plymouth (Gurnet) Light
Courtesy US Coast Guard

became known as Gurnet Point Light in Plymouth, Massachusetts. It was the first station built with twin towers in the nation.

Soon after, John Thomas was called to serve in the Revolutionary War, leaving his wife, Hannah, to handle all the responsibilities at the lighthouse. Having to tend to the lighthouse all by herself technically made Hannah America's first female lighthouse keeper. John Thomas became a major general, but he never came back from the war. Smallpox spread through his troops as they were marching into Canada to fight against British strongholds there. Thomas died of the disease on June 2, 1776, outside of Montreal, Canada.

Hannah Thomas, a widowed mother of three young children, dairy farmer, and lighthouse keeper, fought for her rights as the rightful owner of the beacon on the gurnet. As a prosperous business owner, she challenged the government of Massachusetts when it attempted to take away her rights as keeper of the lighthouse on her property. She remained dedicated to tending the light and even helped hire a local resident, Nathaniel Burgess, to act as keeper ten years later, in 1786.

After the American Revolution, the lighthouse was refurbished and placed back in service in 1790. The new U.S. government ceded the light, and Hannah's son, John Thomas, took over as keeper. Hannah faithfully continued her service at the lighthouse with her son for many years afterward, until his appointment ended in 1812. The lighthouse is the oldest surviving wooden beacon in the United States.

Hannah is believed to haunt the keeper's house and the lighthouse itself, as sightings have been reported for many years following her death in 1819. Many have claimed to have seen the apparition of a woman sitting in front of the window of the keeper's building as if she were waiting for someone, then disappearing. She has also been seen in the tower lantern room of the lighthouse.

In 1994, two photographers from Florida, Bob and Sandra Shanklin, spent a night at Gurnet Point Light in the keeper's home. Bob Shanklin reported that during the night, he awoke to see the ghost of a sad-faced woman hovering over his sleeping wife. The woman wore colonial-era clothing and had long dark hair; her cheeks were sunken, and her expression was very sorrowful. As Bob watched her, he felt no threat, only her sadness. He noticed the light rays from the lighthouse illuminating the room multiple times. He glanced briefly at the light and then turned back toward the figure, but she had vanished.

The Plymouth Light Station is also thought to be haunted by a young woman named Eunice Burgess, who leaped to her death at age 16 from a nearby cliff after her father, Joseph, forbade her from marrying her lover, a local soldier. This cliff has since been called "Lovers Rock."

Current tower of Plymouth (Gurnet) Light

Army of Two: Fife and Drum Music

Scituate Light, Scituate, Massachusetts

By the late 18th century, the town of Scituate had become a significant contributor to the fishing industry thanks to its rather small yet sheltered harbor. However, some mariners who entered the harbor occasionally found themselves grounded in its shallow waters at low tide, or on its changing mud flats. Scituate Lighthouse was constructed in Massachusetts in 1811, just before the War of 1812 erupted between the emerging United States and Britain. Scituate's first Keeper, Simeon Bates, held the position until he died in 1834. He and his wife lived at the lighthouse with their nine children. Two of their daughters, Abigail and Rebecca Bates, gained recognition for their brave efforts to protect the town from a British invasion.

Scituate Lighthouse over breakwater in harbor.

During the War of 1812, British warships frequently raided coastal towns in New England. On June 11, 1814, British forces burned and plundered several ships in Scituate's Harbor. Keeper Bates fired a small cannon twice at a British warship as it left the harbor, but the shots missed, and the ship sailed away

46

without retaliation. After the incident, the townspeople, including the keeper and his family, stayed alert for another possible invasion of the town.

On September 1, 1814, most of the Bates family went into town to gather supplies and visit other relatives. The oldest daughter, 21-year-old Rebecca, and her younger 15-year-old sister Abigail were left in charge of the lighthouse. The sisters enjoyed playing the fife and drum together, and Rebecca could perform four military tunes, including "Yankee Doodle."

Later that day, the sisters spotted a British warship in the distance, anchored just outside Scituate Harbor. They noticed two boats carrying "redcoats" departing from the ship and rowing toward the mainland. Realizing that firing shots from a musket at the lighthouse might only wound a couple of soldiers as they approached, and fearing an imminent British attack on the town, Rebecca decided to adopt a different tactic. She grabbed her fife and instructed Abigail to take her drum. The two girls ran into a nearby grove of cedar trees, hidden from the view of the British, and began to play "Yankee Doodle," as they had practiced many times before. They played louder and louder, hoping to convince the British that a local militia regiment was gathering nearby to protect the town.

They succeeded in deceiving the commander of the British warship, as they observed the boats returning to the ship and the vessel beginning to sail out of sight. The famed "Lighthouse Army of Two" became local heroes for preventing a British naval force from pillaging the town.

In their later years, Rebecca and Abigail received pensions from Congress to recognize their heroism. Many years after their deaths, some locals claimed to have seen the two sisters' ghosts. There have also been numerous accounts of fife and drum music being heard outside of the lighthouse.

Scituate Light in front of keeper's building, oldest original quarters.

47

Lighthouse Storm and Ghost Keepers

Minot's Ledge Light, Cohasset, Massachusetts

Minot's Ledge is located south of Boston Harbor, about 2.5 miles from the Cohasset shore. It is a treacherous rocky ledge that has sunken many vessels and claimed countless lives before Minot's Ledge Lighthouse was constructed there in January 1850. The building process took three years, and the structure was hailed as an engineering marvel. It featured an enormous lantern atop a tall 87-foot skeletal iron tower designed to shield the structure and its keepers from the powerful winds and waves. The innovative concept allowed fierce winds and waves to flow through rather than relentlessly battering a solid, enclosed structure, which was the typical design for most other lighthouses.

However, issues began to arise shortly after the tower's completion, accompanied by numerous complaints from its keepers. The first keeper, Isaac Dunham, resigned

Initial Tower of Minot's Ledge Lighthouse
Image Courtesy US Coast Guard

after ten months at Minot's Ledge Light, believing the structure was poorly constructed and fearing for his safety. Constant vibrations from the crashing waves and winds led to visible cracks where holes had been drilled for the pillars. The pillars were loosening, and in January 1851, Keeper John Bennett expressed concerns that the structure would not withstand the winter, as he and his assistants stationed at the beacon would be knocked off their feet when heavy seas battered the structure. His superiors insisted that the tower was safe and maintained that everyone must remain and fulfill their duties.

The keeper had two assistants who enjoyed working at the lighthouse. In response to journalists' questions about the lighthouse's safety, Joseph Wilson, a 20-year-old proud sailor from England, stated in an interview that he would stay as long as Bennett was present. Joseph Antoine was a 25-year-old Portuguese sailor with relatives in the nearby town of Cohasset.

The "Lighthouse Storm" and the Tragedy Afterwards

On Monday morning, April 14, 1851, Keeper Bennett had to go ashore to gather essential supplies and to find another boat to replace one that was lost in a storm the previous week. He left Joseph Antoine and Joseph Wilson to manage the lighthouse in his absence. He was unaware of an approaching storm that would suddenly hit the Massachusetts coast that Monday afternoon with great intensity, preventing the two men from leaving their post.

It became one of the worst storms in New England's recorded history, continuing through that Saturday, April 19. This storm, which made landfall on the New England coastline on Monday, brought all the elements of high winds, rain, hail, and even snow for nearly a week, resulting in devastation all along the eastern seaboard and inland in central and southern New England. Many wharves along the coastlines of New Hampshire and Massachusetts suffered severe damage from high winds, flooding rain, and rising tides. Homes and other buildings were swept into the sea; many boats that were moored in the harbors collided with one another or were dislodged and carried out to sea. Some lives were also lost due to this ferocious storm. Inland, hurricane-force winds tore off roofs and even toppled some church steeples.

By Wednesday afternoon, April 16, the seas continued to surge and pound Minot's Ledge Lighthouse. The only way to reach the shore would have been to descend the 87-foot structure via a rope in their small boat and fight through the dangerous waves for miles to get to the mainland. This task was impossible, so the two had no choice but to endure the storm and hope to survive.

As the seas worsened, the men lit the lantern at five o'clock to help others avoid a perilous fate. By nightfall, the waters swelled from high tides, fierce wind gusts, and torrential rains. The brave men continued their faithful duties, uncertain whether they would survive the night. Anxious locals watched the lantern from the shore as hurricane-force winds, recorded at over 100 miles per hour, relentlessly battered the lighthouse. The two assistant keepers managed to keep the lighthouse lamp burning until 10:00 p.m., as noted by observers on shore. They consistently rang the fog bell until about one o'clock in the morning, when the tower collapsed and was swept away.

One could only imagine the anguish the two men felt as they awaited their fate and the deep sense of loss as the tower began to collapse under the pressure of the devastating waves and winds. Their cries would never be heard in their last moments as the pillars gave way, sending the entire iron structure toppling into the sea, tossing them into their watery graves.

Etching of "Destruction of Minot's Ledge Lighthouse"
Courtesy Library of Congress

Around 4 o'clock on Thursday morning, there was a lull in the storm, and Keeper Bennett went to the beach to check if the tower was still standing. He saw no sign of the tower, only the bent iron pilings where the lighthouse once stood. Plenty of debris had washed up on the shore. As he examined the debris, he noticed that much of it belonged to the lighthouse structure and the keeper's living quarters, including bedding and some clothing. He discovered two life vests washed ashore that appeared to have been worn but may have been removed from the two men by the angry waves.

Joseph Antoine's body was discovered later that day near Nantasket Beach. Two days later, a Gloucester fisherman found a bottle containing a final message from the doomed keepers: "The beacon cannot last any longer. She is shaking a good three feet each way as I write. God bless you all." Months later, in October, Joseph Wilson's body was found washed up about a mile away from the lighthouse site, on nearby Gull Rock with a fractured skull. He was probably struck by debris from the falling lighthouse. Some believe he may have made it to shore alive, but died shortly after from exposure.

By Sunday, April 20, the storm had finally cleared after nearly a week of devastation in New England. It would take many years to assess and rebuild the damage caused by this fierce and destructive storm. It was later named the "Lighthouse Storm" because it was directly responsible for the destruction of Minot's Ledge Lighthouse.

Keeper Bennett oversaw a temporary lightship that would be anchored just off Minot's Ledge, where the original lighthouse once stood. Construction of the new Minot's Ledge Lighthouse began in 1855 and was celebrated as another significant milestone in lighthouse engineering, incorporating lessons learned from the earlier ill-fated structure. Workers on the project were allowed only if they could swim. However, building the new lighthouse progressed slowly. Many of these men were often swept off the rocks by the relentless waves crashing over the ledge, causing other crew members to halt their work to assist their distressed comrades.

Two years into the construction of the lighthouse, the ship *New Empire* crashed against the treacherous ledge, causing significant damage to the structure. Three years later, in 1860, Minot's Ledge lighthouse was finally completed, becoming one of the most expensive lighthouses in history. It is still regarded as one of the greatest engineering feats of the Lighthouse Service. Each April, people remember Joseph Antoine and Joseph Wilson, and many believe their spirits continue to guard the lighthouse as the ghost keepers of Minot's Ledge Light.

Ghost Keepers Assisting Fishermen

Since the tragedy, Minot's Ledge Lighthouse is said to be haunted by the two assistant keepers. Many fishermen claim that during stormy weather, they have seen a man hanging from a ladder on the side of the tower, screaming, "Stay away, stay away," in Portuguese (Joe Antoine was Portuguese). Other local fishermen over the years have reported hearing moans and cries for help coming from the base of the lighthouse. There have also been the sounds of a phantom bell ringing over the waters.

Both Joe Wilson and Joe Antoine once devised a method to signal the end of their shifts with five loud taps that echoed up the long stairway. After their deaths, other keepers stationed at Minot's Ledge Lighthouse reported hearing the five taps reverberating through the stairs at the end of a shift, with no one present below to create the sounds. Still others who stayed at the rebuilt granite lighthouse have reported seeing two shadowy figures, presumably the two assistant keepers, in the lantern room in the middle of the night.

When birds frequently flew overhead, they would dirty the windows, taking much of the day for the keeper to clean. There have been reports from keepers and caretakers regarding the cleaning of these lighthouse windows from bird droppings. Some have mentioned that the task would mysteriously be completed when they gathered the materials to clean the windows. One keeper brought his cat to the tower for companionship. He reported that the cat behaved very strangely near the lantern room, running in circles and yowling.

One of the last keepers stationed at the light was tapping his pipe at his desk when he heard a knock on the wall. He yelled, "What do you want?" The assistant keeper, who had been sleeping in another room, replied, "Why did you wake me up?" Both men realized no one was on the other side of the wall.

Minot's Ledge Light on a foggy morning.

Woman in Scarlet and Playful Keeper

Long Island Head Light, Boston, Massachusetts

Long Island is the longest and largest of the 34 islands in Boston Harbor. Numerous petitions were made for a lighthouse to be constructed on the island due to the increasing number of vessels entering Boston Harbor. In 1818, a committee from the Boston Marine Society submitted their recommendation, as Congress agreed and allocated funds for construction, which was completed in 1819. Long Island Head Lighthouse was later rebuilt in 1844. It became the nation's first lighthouse made of cast iron. Spirits of a former keeper and a woman dressed in red have been seen near or at the lighthouse.

Long Island Head Light, first beacon made of cast iron

Woman in Scarlet

Before the lighthouse was built in early 1776, during the Revolutionary War, the American fleet had blockaded several British vessels in Boston Harbor, which led to intense artillery battles. The British attempted to escape while local Colonial militias continued firing cannonballs at the retreating ships. Aboard one of those vessels were William and Mary Burton, newlyweds at the time. William served as a soldier in the British fleet. During the battle, Mary was struck in the head by a cannonball. Realizing it was a fatal wound, she begged her husband not to bury her at sea before she passed away.

Compassionate colonists responded to William's plea regarding his wife's final wish and permitted her burial on the island. He had no special burial attire except for a scarlet blanket he found, which he carefully wrapped around Mary and sewed it to her body. He then transported her remains to Long Island in the harbor, where he laid his beloved to rest after a brief service.

In 1804, some fishermen were shipwrecked on the island during a storm. When they were rescued, they reported seeing a woman in a red cloak with blood streaming from her head approaching them before disappearing over a nearby hill. Sightings of the "Woman in Scarlet" have been documented over the years, including one in 1891 by a soldier named William Liddell at Fort Strong, which was established on the island shortly after the Civil War. Over the years, various sightings of the ghost of Mary Burton have been reported by lighthouse caretakers and fishermen.

Former Keeper Makes His Funeral Fun

Keeper Edwin Tarr was the last custodian of Long Island Head Light, situated on a hill. He began his service at the lighthouse in 1906. Renowned for his sense of humor and dedication, he was a favorite among visitors to the island. On January 8, 1918, the keeper passed away while seated in a chair, gazing out at the water.

His funeral took place in the keeper's house atop the hill next to the lighthouse. As the small ceremony unfolded, a storm approached the area, blanketing the island and its surroundings in sleet. The four pallbearers began to leave the house, carrying the keeper's coffin as they tried to navigate the slippery slope to the dock. The icy coating was too much for the anxious men, and they quickly lost control of the coffin, which slipped from their grasp and started to slide down the path. The four men jumped onto the wooden casket as it gained speed, riding it like a sled until it finally came to a stop at the island's wharf. Relieved and trying not to laugh, the guests resumed the service without any further surprises.

Many believe that Keeper Tarr's ghost still haunts the lighthouse. Reports have emerged of an apparition resembling a man in a vintage keeper's uniform appearing in the lantern room when no one else is around.

Spirits of Boston Harbor Lighthouse

Boston Harbor Light, Boston, Massachusetts

Boston Harbor was deep and large enough to establish itself as the premier American commercial center during colonial times. Any vessels entering the harbor had to navigate between the rugged Brewster Islands in the outer harbor and a mainland peninsula known as Point Allerton in the town of Hull. Harbors, islands, and coastal shores featured early beacons that were not used for navigation but rather to warn islanders, mainland communities, and mariners of approaching enemy ships and pirates.

In 1715, with an ever-increasing amount of shipping traffic entering the harbor, the General Court of Massachusetts passed the Boston Light Bill to construct a beacon specifically for navigational purposes on what we now know as Little Brewster Island. At that time, it was known as Beacon Island, and some speculate that a form of beacon may have been used to alert colonists prior to the construction of Boston Harbor Light. The beacon became active on September 14, 1716, with George Worthylake serving as its first keeper. His family grew up on the islands and he was also employed as a harbor master.

Boston Harbor Light in early morning fog (Graves Light in background).

Tragedies Follow the First Lighthouse

America's oldest lighthouse station, established in 1716, experienced a tumultuous early history that led many to believe that the lighthouse and island were cursed. In November 1718, Keeper Worthylake, accompanied by his wife Ann and daughter Ruth, went ashore with one of their servants, George Cutler, to attend a church service and gather supplies, including his pay. They had left their teenage daughter Ann with her friend Mary Thompson, and slaves Shadwell and Dina on the island to maintain the lighthouse during their absence. Their other children were on nearby Lovell's Island with relatives. The Worthylakes were Congregationalists, and church services were not mandatory in Colonial Massachusetts.

The next morning, on Monday, November 3, while returning to the lighthouse, they stopped at a sloop anchored about a mile and a half from Little Brewster Island after being invited aboard by their friend, John Edge. They spent an hour of eating and some light drinking, and invited him to join them at the lighthouse. He accepted the invitation, and they set out in their sloop.

The seas were growing choppy as gusts of wind surged from an impending storm. The lighthouse sloop navigated the channel and anchored a few hundred yards from the lighthouse, safely distanced from the treacherous rocks of Little Brewster Island. Young Ann Worthylake and her friend Mary watched from the shore. It was just after noon, and Ann instructed Shadwell to take their small wooden boarding boat out to ferry the group to the island.

All passengers climbed into the boat as Shadwell began heading toward the shore. Suddenly, the two girls watched in horror as the overloaded vessel, now halfway to the lighthouse, capsized, tossing all six occupants into the frigid waters. Ann stared in disbelief as her father, mother, and older sister cried out in terror, desperately trying to grasp the overturned small craft alongside the other three men. However, they all succumbed to the icy November seas and drowned. Soon, a deafening silence fell, leaving only the sounds of the howling winds as the lifeless bodies floated in the churning surf.

The three family members who died that day were later buried on Copps Hill in Boston, beneath a distinctive triple headstone where Ruth was centered between her parents on either side. The young stonemason who crafted this unique headstone, John Guad, would marry Ann Worthylake a month later.

View the Worthylakes may have seen of the lighthouse before the tragedies.

Robert Saunders became the second interim keeper while Captain John Hayes awaited his debated nomination for the position. Two weeks after the tragedies, on Friday, November 14, 1718, Saunders and two other men, John Chamberlain and another named Braddock, were returning through treacherous, white-capped waters from a call about a ship believed to be in distress, but it turned out to be a false signal.

After anchoring their ship, they rowed their small boat toward the rocky shore and were within a few hundred feet of the lighthouse when a large wave caused the boat to capsize, spilling all three into the icy waters. The trio struggled to swim to shore, but exposure began to overwhelm Saunders and Braddock as they slipped beneath the waves in exhaustion and drowned. Chamberlain continued to fight for his life, swimming toward the island with all the strength he could muster. He felt a rocky crag just below the surface of the water and was able to rest just long enough to regain his strength, allowing him to reach the island safely.

While Saunders was technically not in service as an official lighthouse keeper- only serving as the interim keeper until the Council appointed Hayes- he was honored as the second keeper of Boston Light. This respectful action provided financial help for his family.

Spirits Around Boston Harbor Light

After this second incident, some people surmised the lighthouse and island might be cursed. Since then, many strange noises and sightings of apparitions have been reported at Boston Light and around the island. It is believed that

George Worthylake, along with other spirits, has never really left the lighthouse over the years.

In 1947, Russell Anderson served as a Coast Guard keeper at Boston Light with his wife Mazie and their three children. One day, while walking along the shore, she heard footsteps behind her but saw no one when she turned around. That night, as she tried to sleep, she sensed a presence in the room, and later, she heard strange, maniacal laughter coming from the boathouse. Although she wasn't familiar with the story of the Worthylake tragedy, she heard the voice of a young girl sobbing and calling out "Shadwell, Shadwell" near the fog signal house by the dock .

Later, she would report in Yankee Magazine that one early November day, the other caretakers went ashore, leaving the Andersons alone to tend the beacon. Russell Anderson fell ill with a fever and went to bed shortly after noon. As the fog began to roll in that evening, Mazie went to tell her husband to start the fog signal engines, but suddenly, they activated on their own and started bellowing over the harbor. She then headed to the tower to turn on the light, and astonishingly, the lighthouse lantern lit up by itself. Additionally, she observed a mysterious figure outlined in the lantern room.

Dennis Dever, the Coast Guard officer in charge at Boston Light during the late 1980s, reported some unusual occurrences at the station. While working in the boathouse, he tuned his radio to a rock station. Often, when no one else was around, the station would mysteriously switch to classical music. He and other Coast Guard crew members attributed these events to "Old George" Worthylake.

One day, while in the keeper's kitchen and gazing out the window at the tower, Dever noticed a man in the lantern room. This was alarming, as the only other person on the island was his assistant in the next room. From a distance, it appeared that the figure at the top of the tower was dressed in an old-fashioned keeper's uniform. He hurried to the tower and climbed the stairs, only to discover the lantern room empty. Tools often went missing, and various pieces of equipment or furniture were frequently rearranged.

Sally Snowman, the last keeper of the lighthouse, reported that some of her Coast Guard Auxiliary personnel and volunteers at Boston Light, known as watchstanders, had seen a woman at dusk standing at the top of the tower with long, flowing hair and a white nightgown. One volunteer, attempting to sleep on the couch in the living room during a rainstorm, where a stairway led to the second floor, saw a faint apparition of a woman approaching them on the stairs above before disappearing.

The Ghost Walk and a Demon Named Hobomock

The Native Quonahassit people have long believed that the granite outcroppings that jut out of the waters near Boston Light are inhabited by a demon named Hobomock. This demon is said to stir up fierce winds along the coast and curse anyone who ventures into its territory. The rocks are infamous for damaging ship hulls and claiming lives, and the area has been responsible for numerous shipwrecks, even with Boston Light in operation.

These rocky shoals extend about six miles to the east of Boston Harbor Light, reaching around the Boston Harbor Islands, including Spectacle Island, Georges Island, and the surrounding waters. In this region, there appears to be some barrier of sound waves, as they are unable to penetrate. When ships sail into this "Ghost Walk," as it is now known, the bell of Boston Light cannot warn them of danger. They cannot hear foghorns or tolling bells. This phenomenon may explain why there has been a substantial number of accidents and fatalities in this area, dating back to the 1780s! This auditory anomaly perplexed even MIT researchers, who spent a summer studying the mystery on Little Brewster Island. The sound simply cannot penetrate this invisible force.

Area to the left (east) of Boston Harbor Light known as the "Ghost Walk."

Phantom Foghorn and Cottage Ghosts

Bakers Island Light, Salem, Massachusetts

Baker's Island is part of a cluster of 15 islands known as the Miseries, located about five miles from Salem Harbor on the Massachusetts North Shore. In addition to the recently renovated lighthouse and keeper's residence, the island features summer cottages, a general store, and a pump house. The original Baker's Island Light station, built in 1859, included two range light towers until its shorter counterpart was extinguished and taken down in 1926.

Early Bakers Island Lighthouse with twin towers - fog siren on right side.
Courtesy US Coast Guard

The Phantom Foghorn

In 1907, a powerful new siren replaced the old fog bell. When it was first aimed at the inner island, it was so loud that the farm animals grazing on the islanders' properties fled as far away from the source as possible. After some complaints, the siren was redirected toward the water, and the community expressed their gratitude. The fog siren remained in use until it was replaced by an air horn in 1959. In July 1967, the horn sounded for over 324 hours—nearly half of that month—due to foggy weather conditions.

Throughout its history, this lighthouse's fog signal has been known to inadvertently sound off in the middle of the night on many clear evenings, seemingly to annoy Coast Guard personnel and visitors. No one knows why this occurs, and many staff members believe it is a ghost that enjoys playing tricks on its guests. This entity seems to take pleasure in disturbing the sleep of the lighthouse caretakers and summer residents (and winter caretakers) on the island by activating the foghorn. It sometimes fails to operate when it's supposed to on foggy nights, yet it works perfectly fine during the day.

A unique story about this foghorn's mysterious bellowing took place in 1898. A group of former lighthouse keepers gathered on the island for a special event. While they waited on the pier for their ferry to arrive that night to take them back to the mainland, they heard the foghorn sounding loudly. Tragically, a violent storm struck during their boat ride home. Their ferry capsized, and all but one of the lighthouse keepers drowned.

Andy Jerome, from the Bakers Island Association, who served as caretaker from 1983 to 1987, recalls the foghorn sounding "for no reason on crystal-clear nights." He reported the issue to the Coast Guard multiple times, but when repairmen came to inspect the device, they could never find anything wrong. According to Jerome, the foghorn never "acted up" during the day; it only malfunctioned in the dead of night.

Grounds of Bakers Island Lighthouse with restored keeper's house and tower.

The Cottage Ghosts

Many of the old summer cottages are said to be haunted as well. The Chase Cottage, the largest building on the island, has reportedly been haunted for years. Family members have claimed to see shadowy figures darting through the dimly lit halls, and at least one individual asserts having encountered an evil presence in the house.

Currently there is still no electricity on the island, except for the lighthouse, so gaslight is still used. Paranormal investigators were invited by owners of some of the cottages to investigate the strange occurrences. When the team arrived with their equipment to measure the area around the cottages for activity, they quickly found there was no electricity available to plug their many special devices into. Ooops!

Most paranormal activity near the Baker's Island cottages occurs during the winter months when the island is uninhabited. Caretakers have reported hearing sounds resembling a party coming from Chase Cottage. At Wells Cottage, workmen have encountered a "kissing ghost" that makes strange sounds. Lights are sometimes seen at the Nicholson house and in the general store when both are closed for the winter season.

For the most part, the caretakers of Baker's Island accept that dealing with the supernatural is simply part of the job. However, on cold winter nights when the temperature drops well below zero and the caretaker, snug in his bed, is awakened by the relentless blowing of the foghorn, Andy Jerome declares, "Then you lose patience with the ghosts real fast!"

Birds swarming around Bakers Island Light tower.

Haunted Lighthouses in New Hampshire

There are five active lighthouses in New Hampshire. Two of these beacons are located along the small eighteen miles of coastline, and are considered to be haunted. One stands on the mainland in Portsmouth, while the other is on one of the Isles of Shoals. The other three lighthouses were built on Lake Sunapee, situated about two hours away on the western side of the state, and are not considered to be haunted.

Portsmouth has always been and continues to be an important shipping and trade port. Portsmouth Harbor Light guides fishermen, shipping vessels, and tourists through the treacherous currents of the Piscataqua River in and out of Portsmouth. The beacon is haunted by multiple spirits including a friendly keeper who loved life at the lighthouse during his lifetime and continues to enjoy hanging around the beacon, even after death.

The second lighthouse is on White Island, also known as the Isles of Shoals Lighthouse. It is located about six miles from the nearest mainland, and ten miles from Portsmouth Harbor. This lighthouse was constructed among a series of dangerous rocky islands called the Isles of Shoals. The lighthouse and island are rumored to be haunted by a female spirit believed to be the pirate Blackbeard's wife. On nearby Smuttynose Island, just a short distance from White Island Light, a botched burglary attempt went awry, resulting in two murders. The spirits of the victims still haunt the island.

Ghost of Blackbeard's Wife

White Island (Isles of Shoals) Light, Rye, New Hampshire

The Isles of Shoals are comprised of a cluster of nine rocky islands about six miles off the New Hampshire and southern Maine coasts. The ownership of these islands is split between both border states, with four islands in New Hampshire, and five in Maine. The only lighthouse in the Isles of Shoals was constructed on White Island, on the New Hampshire side, in 1821. Over the years, the islands became a source of media attention and even tourism with stories of shipwrecks, murders, and even treasure left by Blackbeard the pirate.

Fishing trawler passes by White Island (Isles of Shoals) Light.

Over 100 years before the lighthouse was built, Edward Teach, known as the pirate Blackbeard, is believed to have visited the Isles of Shoals with one of his wives around 1715. Although Ocracoke Inlet in North Carolina served as his home base, Teach also terrorized the New England coast. His beard, which was entirely black and thoroughly covered his face, gave him a fearsome look to those who met him. He never took marriage seriously; over the course of his life, he had fourteen wives and fathered at least forty children.

There have been many claims that Edward Teach left part of his treasure on a nearby island that is a short distance from the current White Island Light. It was initially known as Londoner's Island and now called Lunging Island. This island was ideal, serving as a British trading post in the 17th century, where boats could easily come and go. After leaving a rather large amount of silver bars on the island, he departed, making his wife on this particular voyage promise to stay near the treasure until he returned. However, he never came back, as he was captured and killed in North Carolina.

Despite numerous searches, no treasure has ever been found; however, witnesses have observed the appearance of a female apparition over the centuries. Some believe she may have been the wife of a lesser-known pirate, while others think she could be someone who perished in a shipwreck. Over the years, she evolved into the figure of Blackbeard's spouse. This apparition appears on White Island and other nearby islands as a tall woman cloaked in a dark coat with long, flowing blonde hair. She has been seen on the rocks, gazing out at the water as if searching for her husband, shouting, "He will return."

Rocky shore by White Island Light.

During the Blizzard of 1978, one of New England's most historic and severe snowstorms, a Coast Guardsman was securing and fastening items around the boathouse by the lighthouse to prevent them from being washed away. At the blizzard's peak, while endangering his life, a ghostly female figure appeared before him, saying, "Don't worry; everything will be fine."

In 1980, another Coast Guardsman found himself inside the covered walkway linking the lighthouse tower to the keeper's building during a severe storm. He heard a woman's voice warning him of impending danger.

Consequently, screeching, human-like sounds have been reported from White Island; however, many believe these sounds originate from the snowy white owls that inhabit the area and emit a shrill cry when disturbed.

Spirits of Humorous Keeper And...

Portsmouth Harbor Light, Portsmouth, New Hampshire

Portsmouth Harbor Lighthouse was built in 1771 on the site of Fort William and Mary, one of the early forts established by the British in 1631. It was the first lighthouse in the American colonies that was built north of Boston. This fort played a role in one of the early acts of rebellion against the British when patriots stole ammunition one night to be used for the Battle of Bunker Hill in Boston. The British occupied both the fort and the lighthouse during the American Revolution. After the war, the fort was renamed Fort Constitution.

View of Fort Constitution and keeper's house from the Portsmouth Light tower.

The lighthouse aided countless ships during storms that battered the rocky coastline. However, many others still wrecked on the shores outside the harbor or became ensnared in the treacherous tidal currents of the deep Piscataqua River. The fort and lighthouse, located on New Castle Island on the outskirts of Portsmouth, provided refuge for those rescued and in need of assistance. It also became a resting place for those who had perished, including those who died in service there. Since then, numerous ghost sightings, noises from shipwrecked souls, and accounts of Keeper Joshua Card happily tending the lighthouse have emerged in the area.

66

America's Oldest Keeper at Retirement

Joshua K. Card was one of the most famous lighthouse keepers in life and afterward. His father was a mariner, and of course, Joshua followed in his father's footsteps, starting as a cabin boy on a schooner with his father serving as First Mate at the age of 12. He became a seasoned sailor until he turned 27. When his father left to sail in the late 1840s for the gold fields of California, Joshua decided to work at the Portsmouth Naval Shipyard for good pay. He later started a business transporting goods between New Castle and Portsmouth as work dwindled at the Navy Yard.

In 1867, with a growing family, he accepted the keeper position at the remote Boon Island lighthouse in southern Maine, where he stayed for six years. However, he grew tired of the isolation at Boon Island and missed the active life around Portsmouth.

In 1872, a tidal wave swept over the island without warning, taking all the boats except one small vessel. Water flooded the lighthouse and keeper's building, rising at least two feet and covering everything while destroying most of the furniture. Card and his family climbed to the top of the tower to wait out the flood and survived the ordeal.

In 1874, he was offered the keeper position at Portsmouth Harbor Light in New Hampshire, which he graciously accepted so he could spend more time with his family. He loved life around the fort, the lighthouse itself, and his neighbors from New Castle Island and Portsmouth, as he was born on New Castle. A longtime resident of the area, he served from 1874 to 1909, one of the longest tenures for a keeper at the same lighthouse and the lengthiest at Portland Harbor Light. Card was also known for his great sense of humor. As part of his uniform, Card wore a cap with the letter "K" surrounded by a wreath. When visitors or locals frequently asked him what the letter stood for, he would reply, "Why Captain, of course."

Keeper Joshua Card
Courtesy New Castle Historical Society

Keeper Card, like many other dedicated lighthouse keepers, seldom took time off, as he cherished all aspects of maintaining the lighthouse and attending to its needs. He maintained the light for years without taking a single day off. He remained at the lighthouse for over 35 years, and during his tenure he only failed to light the lamp 11 times. This was a remarkable testament to his dedication. When he retired in 1909 at the age of 86, he was the oldest lighthouse keeper in the United States. He passed away shortly after his retirement in 1911; he had devoted a combination of forty-two years of service at Maine's Boon Island Light (1867 to 1874) and New Hampshire's Portsmouth Harbor Lighthouse (1874 to 1909). A newspaper writer remarked, "Card's demeanor was knowledgeable; he was punctual to the minute, possessed a kind sense of humor, and was always courteous to his neighbors and visitors to the lighthouse." He was laid to rest about a mile away from the lighthouse.

Waterside view of Portsmouth Harbor Light station.

Spirits in the Night

Joshua Card, even after death, seems to be connected to many of the area's ghost stories. Although he retired due to an apparent slight stroke, and some reports suggest he retired against his will at the age of 86, his spirit has been seen and heard for many years since his death in 1911. Recently reported sightings of Card's ghost include personnel stationed at the nearby Coast

Guard building observing a "shadowy figure" roaming the grounds at night, as well as hearing footsteps between 2 a.m. and 3 a.m. leading to the watchtower of the central Coast Guard building, and hearing footsteps on the stairs of the lighthouse. Coast Guardsmen working on the first floor of the keeper's building have reported hearing footsteps going back and forth on the second floor when no one was present there.

Once, the chairperson of the Friends of Portsmouth Lighthouse was painting in the lantern room of the lighthouse. He heard a voice say, "How are you doing?" When he yelled down his response, there was no one in sight.

There have been sightings of a man in an old keeper's uniform from the early 1900s, standing in front of the keeper's house for a brief time, and then disappearing. One time, a woman was visiting the station, she reported seeing a figure in broad daylight standing on the wooden walkway in front of the lighthouse, wearing an "old-fashioned" keeper's uniform. She though it was a great idea to have someone giving tours in costume, but then she realized that he just vanished. Quite shaken, she walked over to the nearby Coast Guard Station to describe her experience and noticed photos of Keeper Card, identifying him as the person she had seen in uniform.

Spirits have also been heard and observed who may have perished at the lighthouse due to the numerous shipwrecks in the area or from sickness. Coast Guardsmen saw a woman in a white gown walking along the wall at night on their closed-circuit monitors. Fearing for her safety, a group ran out to speak to the lady; however, they found no one there when they went out to investigate.

Even with the grounds continuously monitored by closed-circuit TV systems, personnel at the Coast Guard station also reported discovering bare footprints of an adult and a child on the helicopter landing pad. They seemed to have appeared out of nowhere and faced each other near the center of the pad, then tracked together about 30 yards behind one of the buildings on the base and into the water. The footprints remained for three days, with those observing the tracks commenting on their rather oily appearance.

Another incident involves a group that were taking a nighttime tour of Fort Constitution. One of the participants took photos of the lighthouse, and in some of the finished prints, a "greenish mist" appears, circling the area with no other light visible or any reflections from cars or nearby buildings.

Investigations of Fort Constitution and Lighthouse Grounds

In the early 2000s, the New England Ghost Project team was contacted to investigate the lighthouse and its grounds. The team brought a medium, Maureen Wood to possibly make contact with any spirits. No information was provided to her to avoid any bias in the investigation. They gathered intriguing EVPs, or electronic voice phenomena, which act as a filtering device on background noise. After midnight, they recorded a voice saying "hello" at a location where no one was present. One team member asked who it was, and the voice replied, "captain," which was how Joshua Card referred to himself.

Tower staircase of
Portsmouth Light.

A short time later, they discovered a highly fluctuating EMF (Electronic Magnetic Field) behind the keeper's building. Maureen was able to contact a female spirit who claimed to be a companion of "the keeper." After asking a few questions, they concluded that the spirit was from the same era as Keeper Joshua Card, who remained a bachelor in his later years after his wife, Dolly, passed away in 1882, suggesting she may have been dating the keeper.

The lighthouse keeper's building was constructed in 1872, but it has since been converted into offices. Over the years, Coast Guard members reported hearing sounds of footsteps on the second floor in a sealed-off area. Maureen made contact with a friendly, peaceful female entity who had recently passed away and expressed a desire to remain at the lighthouse station, explaining that she had spent her life around lighthouses. Maureen could see in her dream state that the spirit held a bouquet of flowers with large pink buds and extended her other hand as if offering a hug. She asked if there was anything else the entity wanted to say, and the spirit whispered a "thank you" to everyone. The medium then temporarily lost consciousness and fell to the floor, knocking over a chair. The spirit was asked to leave at that moment while Maureen slowly awakened from her trance.

Upon evaluating the events, the team concluded that the female entity was Connie Small, who had recently passed away at the age of 103. She was well-known for her book, "The Lighthouse Keeper's Wife," and had spent 26 years tending to lighthouses in New England, including some of the most remote ones along the coast. Connie and her husband, Ellsworth Small, were the last civilian lighthouse keepers at Portsmouth Harbor Light.

The pink flowers were given to her by one of the team members, Jeremy D'Entremont, a noted lighthouse historian and chairperson of the Friends of Portsmouth Lighthouse organization. The experience of contacting Connie was a shocking revelation for everyone in the group, some knew this remarkable woman personally in life. After viewing the recorded video, members could discern a female face on the floor near the chair that had been knocked over.

On another night, during a visit when no one was at the tower, one of the members climbed the stairs to the top and asked, "Do you enjoy our presence here?" The recorded response was, "Yes." Another member outside made a recording where he said "I think you should check the light." After a brief pause, a response came back as saying "OK."

Crashing waves from coastal storm by Portsmouth Harbor Light.

The fort next to the lighthouse was originally built by the British nearly 500 years ago in 1631, and is one of the oldest in the country. It was named Fort William and Mary, and over the years was a trading port, a target of warfare, and a military training ground. It was also a center of rebellion before the American Revolution. After the war, the colonists changed its name to Fort Constitution.

On July 4, 1809, damp ammunition casings were left out in the sun to dry. Sergeant Allen fired his cannon to celebrate the holiday in honor of Walbach, the commanding officer, and his guests, as was customary. A spark carried by the wind ignited the powder in one of the casings, resulting in a massive explosion. A chain reaction caused seventeen cartridges to detonate, killing three soldiers, one civilian, and three boys. Six soldiers and several civilians suffered severe wounds from burns and shrapnel in this horrific incident.

Psychic John Holland was invited to conduct a walk through, concentrating on Fort Constitution rather than the lighthouse. He received no information regarding the fort's history. As he led his group around the old fort, he consistently saw the number four (July 4th?) in his mind and sensed a strong smell of gunpowder and smoke. He felt that several deaths had taken place.

Some time later, the New England Ghost Project also conducted a walk through of the fort, and Maureen Wood, the medium accompanying them, sensed the same feelings and smells that John Holland had experienced years earlier. She received no prior information but when entering the gates she perceived that it resembled a war scene with bodies dismembered by an explosion and much screaming. She began communicating with a spirit overwhelmed by guilt from that period of 1809. It was very distraught, unable to understand why it had survived when others did not, and wished it could have found a way to prevent the accident.

The Ghost Project, during another visit, invited some locals to bring their cameras and assist with an investigation on a nighttime tour of Fort Constitution. One participant lingered behind the group and captured images in the darkness inside the fort. Upon reviewing the developed prints, one image displayed a greenish streak stretching from the left to the right side of the front gates, with a clear background suggesting no camera movement; upon closer inspection, it resembled the shape of a leg. The same image revealed three moving green and yellow lights, also set against a sharp background. Some believe these lights may signify a type of portal that spirits could use to travel between worlds.

The ghost-seeking team from the show "Ghost Hunters" visited to film any strange occurrences and help explain some of the unusual activities. The area was completely closed to the public. As the ghost-seekers investigated and recorded throughout the night inside Portsmouth Harbor Lighthouse, Fort Constitution, and the keeper's quarters, they captured some intriguing footage as evidence.

Most experiences seemed to occur inside the lighthouse. Two of the three teams heard strange noises there, like footsteps on the stairs, while all the team members were in the tower. Two female team members even communicated with the entity by knocking out a "cut and a shave" sequence, and the entity responded. Evidence of the knocking response sounds and footsteps was recorded on video.

Years later, the Souhegan Paranormal team from Nashua, New Hampshire, was invited to investigate. While on the second floor of the keeper's house, the team members heard a voice say, "Mary, Mary."

Leander White replaced Joshua Card as the keeper, serving from 1909 to 1915 alongside his wife, Elizabeth. They had a daughter named Mary, who married the next keeper, Henry Cuskley. Mary passed away in 1938, while Henry remained at the lighthouse until his death in 1941. He had served as keeper for about 26 years, from 1915 to 1941. The voice, believed to be female, may have been the mother calling out to her daughter, Mary.

In the basement of the keeper's quarters, the team heard some voices and a slamming of a door, with no wind drafts to cause the incident, which was also captured on tape. Some noises were heard outside the fort, but nothing could be identified as possibly paranormal.

The reported spirits seen and heard around the fort grounds, the keeper's house and Coast Guard station, and near the lighthouse are peaceful entities and there is no evidence of any malicious intentions. Keeper Joshua Card's ghost appears to enjoy the attention as he continues to visit the lighthouse on select nights. He still cares for the operation of the light, the company of visitors and caretakers, and helping to guide mariners home.

Smuttynose Island Murders

Smuttynose Island (Near White Island Light), Kittery, Maine

The Isles of Shoals consist of nine islands; most are very close to each other, two were connected by breakers. Four islands are along the New Hampshire border, while the remaining five are on the Maine border. White Island Lighthouse is located on the New Hampshire side, and Smuttynose Island is situated on the Maine border. In 1873, a burglary went awry on Smuttynose Island, not far from White Island Light, resulting in two murders. Since then, the area has been haunted by the spirits of the victims and the killer.

White Island (Isles of Shoals) Light (circa 1888)
Library of Congress

Norwegian immigrants John and Maren Hontvet arrived in Portsmouth, New Hampshire, in 1868 to make a living fishing off the Isles of Shoals. They settled on Smuttynose Island, where they appreciated the privacy and solace it offered, away from the bustling fishing docks of Portsmouth. Maren cherished the tranquility while maintaining the house they had found on the island. They had a small dog named Ringe, who comforted Maren while John was away.

Every day at dawn, John would sail his schooner, the *Clara Bella*, to the fishing grounds, pull in his trawl lines, and then head to the market in nearby Portsmouth to sell his catch. He would buy bait for the following day's trip and return home usually in the late afternoon. His persistence and hard work earned him a successful business, and his friends and other fishermen respected him in the area.

Louis Wagner, a loner in his late twenties, fished around the nearby islands of the Isles of Shoals. No one knew much about his past, and many found him secretive. He was a strong able-bodied individual who had a bit of a drinking problem. He had started a relationship with the Hontvets as working neighbors, and within two years, the Norwegian couple had become close friends with Wagner. They knew he was barely making a living fishing alone and helped ensure he was fed and clothed.

In May 1871, Maren's sister, Karen Christensen, arrived from Norway to begin a new life after losing her true love. She found work as a live-in maid at a hotel owned by the renowned poet and author Celia Thaxter on Appledore Island, the largest of the Isles of Shoals, next to Smuttynose Island.

As John's business continued to thrive, he realized he needed more help on the *Clara Bella* and hired Louis Wagner in June 1872. He was also given an upstairs room in the Hontvets' house, as they wanted him to feel like part of their family. However, by October, other family members from Norway joined the couple on the island. John's brother Matthew arrived in October, and Maren's brother, Ivan Christensen, along with his new wife, Anethe, came shortly thereafter. This created a rather cramped situation. With the added family members, John had more help than he required.

Portrait of Louis Wagner
Courtesy Wikimedia Commons

Ivan and Matthew went to work for John, while Anethe assisted Maren with household duties. Louis Wagner stayed with the Hontvets for over a month before deciding it was time to leave. He found work on another fishing schooner, the *Addison Gilbert*, and left Smuttynose in November to secure a room onshore and pay rent to a couple named Jonsen. However, the ship was wrecked in a storm shortly after, leaving him with meager wages working along the Portsmouth docks. He earned so little that he barely managed to cover the rent for the Jonsens. By the end of February 1873, he was destitute; his clothes were torn, and he was forced to survive on food scraps. Believing that John Hontvet had stashed about $600 (value of $15,000 today) at the house to purchase a new boat, Wagner came up with a plan to steal the money while the women were asleep and the men were overnight at the Portsmouth waterfront.

On the morning of March 5, 1873, John, Matthew, and Ivan set sail from Smuttynose to trawl for fish. They had heard that an early train with fresh bait was scheduled to arrive in Portsmouth, but if it didn't, they would simply wait on the shore overnight, preparing to bait the hooks for the next day. At sea, they encountered a neighbor and asked him to stop at Smuttynose to inform the women that they were sailing directly to the mainland, favoring the winds so they wouldn't be leaving one of the men on the island, as was their custom, and that they might be home later that evening, depending on when the train was arriving.

When the *Clara Bella* docked in Portsmouth early that evening, Louis Wagner was there to help secure the vessel to the wharf. He asked the men if they planned to return to Smuttynose that night, which seemed odd to them, as they explained that they

Cape Ann Fishing Schooner (1905)
Library of Congress

would head home if the bait arrived on time, but if it were delayed, they would stay in port, bait their trawl lines, and leave for home in the morning. Knowing Louis Wagner needed money, John asked if he wanted to help with baiting the lines, which could take all night, to which Wagner agreed and left the wharf. The conspirator learned that the train would be delayed, ensuring the men would remain at the docks that night.

Cape Ann Fisherman and Dory (1905)
Library of Congress

The cold, moonlit evening was calm, and the sea was quiet with gentle waves. These conditions provided Wagner the chance to steal a dory from a fisherman he knew, named David Burke, around 8 p.m. from the dock at Pickering Street in the city's South End. It was a 10-mile journey from Portsmouth Harbor to Smuttynose Island. He was a strong man and knew it would take less than three hours. John Hontvet had told him that he had made the trip at least 60 times from Portsmouth, along with many others in the fishing community over the years. This fishing boat was sleek in design for easy navigation through the ocean waters, and the outgoing tide was helping to carry him out to sea.

He rowed past Portsmouth Harbor Light on nearby New Castle Island. The island is a short distance from Portsmouth and is connected by rather short, low bridges, allowing locals to walk and fish there easily. The trip would be challenging, but he was determined to complete the 10-mile journey. He was last seen at the docks around 7:30 that night.

At the Hontvet house on Smuttynose Island, Karen, Maren's sister, was staying with the family while preparing to move out. She had planned to leave her job at the hotel to work as a seamstress in Boston. Around 10 p.m., Maren, Karen, and Anethe assumed the men would not return that night. They changed into their nightgowns, and Maren made a bed for Karen in the kitchen, which was warmer than the upstairs bedrooms. She and Anethe then went to an adjoining bedroom.

Hontvet house after the murders took place (circa 1873).
Image Portsmouth Library (Woman not one of the Hontvet family)

Wagner rowed to the island's far side, away from the nearby cove where the *Clara Bella* would have docked, and then hiked to the cottage. The island was blanketed in a thin layer of snow as he watched for several hours until he was certain everyone was asleep. The women had left the door unlocked in case the men returned late that night. Wagner opened the door to the dark kitchen where Karen was sleeping and quietly closed it behind him. Then, he discreetly jammed a piece of wood into the latch of the bedroom door, behind which Maren and Anethe were sleeping. Ringe, their dog, heard Wagner adjusting the latch and began barking at the intruder. Karen instantly woke up and asked, "John? Is that you?" believing it was her brother-in-law.

Maren sat up in bed and called to her sister, "Karen? Is something wrong?" Realizing his identity would soon be uncovered, Wagner panicked and grabbed a chair while the dog continued barking. He struck Karen and persisted in his attack, fully intending to silence her.

Maren jumped out of bed and tried to open the locked door, shouting to her sister, who was struggling to escape from her attacker. Karen was thrown against the bedroom door but managed to free the latch. She fell at Maren's feet, bloodied, as Maren dragged her sister out of Wagner's reach. He punched both women repeatedly while Maren managed to close and barricade the door as he attempted to force his way in.

From the corner of the bedroom, young Anethe froze in shock from the horrific scene in front of her, while Maren yelled to her to run and hide. Still not comprehending what was going on, Anethe climbed out the window and stood barefoot in the snow in front of the house. Maren cried out for her to run, but she remained motionless in the moonlight, too shocked to run. Wagner ran out of the house and grabbed a hatchet axe near the well. Anethe, seeing who the attacker was, yelled, "Louis! Louis!" Her cries were silenced as Wagner, now in a fit of rage, struck two fatal blows to her head with the axe; she was dead.

Maren heard Anethe's cries and saw the shadows of the gruesome act from the bedroom window, but she did not see Wagner's face. She pleaded with her sister, lying beside the bed, to get up and escape with her through the window, but Karen, barely conscious and bloodied from the blows of the chair, could not move. Realizing she had no choice but to save herself, Maren wrapped herself in a heavy skirt and climbed through the window, quietly fleeing the scene with Ringe running alongside her.

At the point of madness, Wagner returned to the house to silence the other two women. He finally broke open the bedroom door as Karen, still dazed, was trying to crawl out the window. He swung the axe wildly at her but missed and smacked it against the windowsill, breaking the handle. Pulling her away from the window as she struggled to get free, he grabbed a handkerchief, twisted it around her neck, and continued to pull it until there was no resistance from her. Her lifeless body slumped to the floor.

In bare feet, Maren ran over the snow-covered ground and looked for Wagner's boat by the cove, which was missing as he had placed it on the other side of the island. She decided to run to the island's far side but had to go past the cottage from a distance, hugging the shore where the snow was washed away by the tides. Grief-stricken and shivering, she reached the island's far side along the water's edge and crawled between some boulders for cover. The pounding of the ocean waves as the tides came in helped to keep her and Ringe undetected, muffling any sounds

Realizing that Maren had escaped, Wagner knew he had to find her to silence her so he wouldn't be exposed. He searched the island, leaving a trail of bloody footprints in the snow. His pursuit proved unsuccessful for the woman who had taken him in with her husband and had provided him food and shelter in his time of need.

He returned to the house, brewed himself a cup of coffee, used the dinnerware to eat some of their food, and searched the rooms for money, leaving bloody fingerprints everywhere. He discovered a wallet containing just 15 dollars and some coins, along with a button that Maren had intended to use to repair a shirt. He pocketed the money (and button) and dragged Anethe's bloodied body back into the kitchen. A clock had fallen off the mantel during the struggle with Karen and had stopped at 1:07. Knowing dawn was approaching, Louis Wagner left the gruesome scene he had created and rowed back toward New Castle Island near Portsmouth, where he disposed of the boat.

It was nearly 8 a.m. before Maren dared to leave her hiding spot. With her feet numb from the cold, she limped across the breakwater linking Smuttynose and tiny Malaga Island. She waved her arms at Jorge Ingerbredsen's children, playing outside their home on nearby Appledore Island, and shouted for help. The children ran to their father, who rowed the quarter mile to rescue Maren. In a soft, grieving voice, Maren explained what had happened at the house. Jorge gathered neighbors with guns to search Smuttynose for the killer. When the group reached the island, they uncovered the horrific deeds committed by Louis Wagner.

Finding no one on Smuttynose, the men returned to Appledore and searched that island. A few hours later, the *Clara Bella* appeared on the horizon, prompting the search party to signal for the fisherman to make a stop there. Seeing the signal from the shore, Matthew and Ivan rowed to Appledore, while

John sailed the schooner to its mooring on Smuttynose. Ivan and Matthew learned about the events on Smuttynose and hurried to the Ingerbredsen house, where they found Maren in a freezing, shocked state. Ivan looked around for his beautiful wife, but tearfully, Maren told him she was "at home."

Ivan and Matthew hurried back to their boat and rowed to Smuttynose. They arrived just as John finished tying up the *Clara Bella*, and together they raced to the house. Ivan pushed open the door and stepped into the kitchen. There, lying on the floor with her long golden hair sprawled in a pool of dried blood, was his beloved Anethe. Covering his face, he dashed out the door and collapsed in tears in the snow.

The three shocked and angry men untied the *Clara Bella* and picked up Maren at Appledore Island. They headed to Portsmouth to inform the police and authorities about the murders committed by Louis Wagner. News spread quickly through this tight-knit fishing community, and his description was telegraphed to police across the coastal states. The evening editions were filled with all the grisly details.

Two men who knew Wagner informed the police they had seen him on nearby New Castle Island around six o'clock that morning. The stolen dory was later discovered in an area known as "Devil's Den" on the back side of the island. Before the boat was taken, the owner had installed new rowlocks for rowing, which appeared worn, presumably from the journey to and from Smuttynose Island.

After returning to his room at the Jonsens' house in Portsmouth, Wagner changed his clothes and hid his blood-stained garments. He took a 9 a.m. train to Boston, where, with the $15 he had stolen, he bought new boots and a suit. He spent the day drinking with women he knew from a boarding house he often frequented. John Hontvet was aware of some of the places in Boston that Wagner stayed and informed the authorities where they might find him. Boston police located and arrested the suspect, who was wearing his new suit over his old torn clothes. He offered no resistance.

The next day, Wagner was transferred from jail to the Boston train depot, where he was to be taken to Portsmouth. An angry crowd of 500 followed him, calling for his death. When news of his arrival reached Portsmouth, thousands filled the streets, demanding that he be executed for his heinous crimes.

The Isles of Shoals are divided between the borders of the states of New Hampshire and Maine. Since the murders happened on Smuttynose Island, which is under Maine's jurisdiction, Wagner would have to stand trial in Maine. Three days later, when he was transferred from the Portsmouth jail to the train, a lynch mob of over 200 fishermen from the islands and the coast waited for the accused and began throwing bricks and stones at him. To help control the angry crowd, the police escort called in soldiers from the nearby Navy base. He was then moved to Alfred, Maine, part of York County, which includes the territory of Smuttynose Island.

The trial of Louis Wagner began on June 9, 1873. In Maren Hontvet's testimony, she acknowledged that on that moonlit night, she didn't see Wagner's face from her window or when she barricaded the door, but she heard Anethe screaming his name just before he killed her. The clock in the house,

Louis Wagner (middle) with Sheriff Cruton (1873)
Courtesy Wikimedia Commons

which had fallen and stopped at 1:07, provided an accurate timeline for the killings. Blood-soaked clothes were found in the bathroom of his rented room. When he was apprehended in Boston, the button belonging to Maren Hontvet was discovered in his shirt pocket. The stolen dory suggested that many miles had been rowed during its theft. The bloody footprints left by boots on the island matched those found in the mud at New Castle; they belonged to Wagner.

The defense sought to persuade the jury that John and Maren Hontvet had framed the accused and were the actual murderers. They also tried to cast doubt on how he could have rowed the nearly 20 miles round trip that night. This prompted some townsfolk to question his guilt, although many fishermen had claimed to have made the same trip. Wagner, however, made unverifiable claims about his whereabouts that night; he had no alibi, as no one came forward to confirm his testimony. The blood stained clothing which he said were from fish were identified as human blood with new technology that had recently been developed. The new suit and boots Wagner purchased with stolen money, along with other circumstantial evidence, contributed to convicting the fisherman of the murders. Throughout the trial, he maintained a passive demeanor. After nine days of testimony and just 55 minutes of deliberation, he was found guilty of the murders and returned to his jail cell in Alfred, Maine.

Just a week later, in June 1873, Wagner escaped from jail by picking the lock and leaving a dummy figure in his cot. As the prison was newly secure, there were rumors that he may have had help, as many believed in his innocence. He made his escape toward the New Hampshire border and evaded authorities for three days before being captured over 40 miles away in Farmington, New Hampshire.

Shortly thereafter, Wagner was transferred to the state prison in Thomaston, Maine, where he awaited execution. Two years later, on June 25, 1875, he was taken to the prison yard and hanged alongside another 28-year-old axe murderer, John Gordon. Gordon had stabbed himself in a suicide attempt the night before and was unconscious at the time of the hanging. After eight minutes of doctors checking his pulse and determining that he was still alive, Louis Wagner finally died on the gallows. He had maintained his innocence until the end.

Anethe Christensen and Karen Christensen, the two victims of Louis Wagner, were buried in a Portsmouth cemetery. A portion of the engravings, presumably written by Anethe's angry husband Ivan, read: "A sudden death to all things call, A warning voice which speaks to all, To all to be prepared to die." Unable to work in the area in his hopeless demeanor of losing Anethe, Ivan returned to Norway. John Hontvet's brother Mathew followed.

Maren and John Hontvet would never return to their house on the Isles of Shoals. Over the years, tourists and locals alike had taken pieces of the wooden shingles and various sections of the house where there were still bloody stains, as souvenirs from this historic event. This made the place uninhabitable, with numerous holes in the walls. Years later, the cottage burned to the ground, its remnants then washed away by the many storms that swept across this rocky island. The Portsmouth Athenaeum still houses the broken-handled axe that Wagner used to carry out his horrific deeds.

The Hontvets moved to Portsmouth, where John continued his career as a fisherman. They welcomed a child, Clara Eleanor Hontvet, born in Portsmouth on January 6, 1877, when Maren was 42. Both faced false rumors about their involvement in the killings from supporters of Wagner's innocence and endured harsh criticism from newspaper writers and conspiracy theorists. The stress and indignity became overwhelming for the once-happy couple, leading Maren and Clara to travel to a village near Oslo, Norway, in the early 1880s. Maren remained in Norway and passed away on June 24, 1887. After surviving several harrowing shipwrecks, John Hontvet decided to stop fishing, remarried in 1888, and took up farming in Portsmouth until his death in 1904.

On Smuttynose Island, near White Island Light, islanders and visitors report hearing moans and screams from the place where the cottage once stood, where Louis Wagner murdered the two women. Many believe the victims are still seeking peace after such a traumatic event. Some have heard a woman crying, thought to be the spirit of Maren or one of the other women. Sightings of Louis Wagner's ghost have also been reported, appearing to search for Maren. Additionally, there is a legend that Louis Wagner returns to the streets of Portsmouth every March 6 around 1 a.m. on the anniversary of the killings, proclaiming his innocence to anyone present who will listen.

Haunted Lighthouses in Maine

The rocky shore and the long, finger-like peninsulas that shape the coast of Maine from Kittery to the Canadian border make Maine's coastline longer than California's. The lighthouses in Maine began with Portland's growth as a major shipping port and the construction of Portland Head Light in 1791, following the American Revolution. Maine has sixty-five lighthouse stations, but only a dozen are on the mainland. The rest of these lighthouses were built on numerous islands, ledges, and reefs that posed dangers for mariners as shipping and fishing traffic increased, particularly with the influx of tourism to areas like Mount Desert, part of present-day Acadia National Park. Fog can form at any time in Maine, especially with the dramatic changes in weather patterns.

Treacherous ledges and shoals, such as Boon Island, required a lighthouse due to the numerous shipwrecks on this small, desolate group of rocks and along the route to Portland. Many lighthouses in Maine were constructed in isolated areas, which could sometimes be overwhelming for the keepers or their wives, such as the female ghost of Boon Island Light, or for those shipwrecked, like the souls of the *Nottingham Galley* lost off Boon Island and those of the ghost ship *Isadore* wrecked near Cape Neddick (Nubble) Light.

Some of these souls were lost in tragic accidents, such as those at Cape Elizabeth Light and Wood Island Light, or succumbed to New England's fierce storms, like the "Ghost Bride of the Beach" near Cape Elizabeth Light. Some keepers were so devoted to their lighthouse stations that their spirits chose to return to the lighthouses they cherished, as noted at Goat Island (Cape Porpoise) Light and Portland Head Light.

Along the Kennebec River in Maine, extending to Pemaquid Point on the rocky shoreline of the Boothbay Region, lighthouses were established on the islands and connecting waterways. These lighthouses were constructed along the lower Kennebec River to guide both commercial sailing and daily steamship traffic into Bath, while also collecting shipments of lumber and other local products from upstream communities.

Many lighthouses in Maine were built in remote locations, which sometimes proved overwhelming for the keepers, like the spirits at Seguin Island Light, or for those shipwrecked nearby, such as the female ghost at Pemaquid Point Light. Some of these souls died in tragic accidents, like the "Lady of the Dusk" at Hendricks Head Light. Some apparitions help mariners in stormy weather, as the "Woman in White" at Ram Island Light. Some keepers, and even their wives, were so devoted to their lighthouse stations that their ghosts have been reported as returning to ensure the lighthouse is well maintained, much like the entities at Burnt Island Light.

The lighthouses in Penobscot Bay and along the northern coast, often called "downeast" Maine, were built to safeguard shipping traffic transporting granite from nearby quarries, as well as lumber and local fishing industries, along a perilous stretch of reefs, ledges, and islands. This area experienced numerous shipwrecks during fierce New England storms, often paired with foggy days each year.

Many of these lighthouses were also built in isolated areas, which sometimes proved overwhelming for those stationed there, such as the entity in the north tower at the remote Matinicus Rock Light. Some individuals met tragic fates, like the restless young spirit at Marshall Point Light, or the construction worker at Bass Harbor Head Light. Some keepers, and even other caretakers, remained at the lighthouse to ensure the lighthouse was taken care of, like the active spirits found at Owls Head Light and the female entity at Narragaugus (Pond Island) Light. Others died unexpectedly at the lighthouse but continued manifesting as playful spirits, like the ghost at Prospect Harbor Light.

Ghost Ship Isadore

Near Cape Neddick (Nubble) Light, York, Maine

Cape Neddick Lighthouse is among the most iconic and photographed beacons in the United States. Located in York, Maine, near the New Hampshire border, it is also referred to as "Nubble Light." The lighthouse stands atop a small rock island known as a "nubble," situated a few hundred feet from the shore. Due to the rocky coastal terrain, many local mariners had called for a lighthouse since the early 1800s. In 1837, a proposal was rejected, citing that there were "already enough lighthouses in the area."

It wasn't until over 35 years later, in 1876, that a lighthouse was finally built, following public outcry over the many shipwrecks that occurred during this period. One of these, the *Isadore* sank during a fierce gale storm claiming all aboard. It was arguably one of the many catalysts for the eventual construction of Cape Neddick Lighthouse. Over the years, mariners and visitors to the area have claimed that on quiet nights, they see the ghost ship sailing near the area where it perished.

Sun breaking through storm clouds by Cape Neddick (Nubble) Lighthouse.

The *Isadore* was a three-masted barque recently built in Kennebunkport, preparing for her maiden voyage to New Orleans. The ship was also chartered to transport cargo from New Orleans across the Atlantic to France afterward. The crew of fifteen ranged in age from a 15-year-old cabin boy to a 53-year-old cook, all of whom hailed from the Kennebunkport area.

Days before the ship set sail, one of the crewmen, Thomas King, vividly dreamed of a shipwreck resembling the *Isadore*, with its crew washed up on the shore. He described this dream to the ship's captain, Leander Foss, pleading to be left on shore. However, the captain warned him that he better be on board when the ship departed, or he would face serious consequences. King had already been paid a month's wages in advance for the trip to their destination.

The night before the *Isadore* sailed, another crewman also dreamed about seven coffins, one of which contained his own body. He also told Captain Foss about his dream and begged him not to let the ship sail the following evening, fearing for the lives of everyone on board. Yet again, Foss refused to listen. The frightened crew member and Thomas King discussed their dreams, fueling King's decision to stay behind.

On Thanksgiving night, the 30th of 1842, the call went out for all crew members to prepare to set sail. Storm clouds had been gathering all day, the winds were beginning to strengthen, and white-capped waves could be seen in the distance. These ominous signs reinforced King's resolve to stay behind. He abandoned his post on the ship and hid in town, fearing the captain's wrath and the ship's fate. Neighbors who heard of his act, ridiculed him for leaving. The other crew members chose to heed the captain's warnings and remained on the ship.

The *Isadore* departed from Kennebunkport as the wind continued to blow fiercely from the northeast, and snow began to fall. By the time the crew rounded Boon Island with its lighthouse flashing to warn of danger, the storm had intensified into gale-force winds. The sea was creating swells over twenty feet high in the blinding snow, tossing the ship closer to the shore between Bald Head Cliffs and Cape Neddick Island, where it crashed against an underwater rock ledge and sank near Maxfield Beach by Wells, Maine.

The wreckage of the ship was discovered the next morning scattered around Cape Neddick Island and the rocky coastline around York. The bodies of seven out of the fourteen crewmen on board the ship were the only ones found washed ashore. One body belonged to the other crewman who had dreamed about the seven coffins and had been too frightened of the captain's wrath to stay on the shore. The body of Captain Ross was never found.

The storm also brought tragedy to nearby Rye, New Hampshire, when the schooner *James Clark*, carrying twenty people, sank near the beach. Many were rescued by a rope set up by the captain and crew, but six passengers lost their lives, including three children. The ship was en route from St. John, New Brunswick, Canada, to Boston.

In 1985, nearly 142 years after the ill-fated *Isadore* set sail off the coast of Maine, an Ogunquit fisherman pulled a 100-pound rudder from the ocean assessed to be from the famed ship. After keeping it for decades, he donated it to the local historical society.

The *Isadore* still appears to be a phantom ship patrolling the bays. Since the day it perished in 1842, there have been sporadic sightings by mariners and visitors just offshore between Boon Island and Cape Neddick Island. Over the years, many fishermen have claimed to see it and have tried to approach the ship, but it always seems to vanish when they are close. Additionally, hotel guests and tourists staying at the shoreline inns, have reported seeing a faint phantom ship, even though most do not know the story behind the tragedy of the *Isadore*.

Waves breaking along shore by Cape Neddick (Nubble) Light.

Souls of the Nottingham Galley

Boon Island Light, York, Maine

The population along the New England coastline dramatically increased in the early eighteenth century. Shipping ports were expanded to accommodate the growing volume of shipping entering the region. Due to New England's frequent and violent storms, numerous shipwrecks occurred on the rocky landmasses and sandbars that dotted the coastline.

Boon Island is a tiny rock island that lies only a few feet above the water at high tide. Measuring roughly 300 feet by 700 feet, it is about six miles from the shoreline of York, Maine. During the seventeenth and eighteenth centuries, shipwrecks often occurred there, where mariners would find themselves stranded on the rocks, only to be washed away from rogue waves breaking over the island or succumbing to prolonged exposure to the elements.

The wreck of the *Nottingham Galley*, though its story is horrific in nature, was one of the early incidents before lighthouses were built that spawned the need for constructing some warning device to help those who may find themselves wrecked on New England's coastline. However, Boon Island is believed to be haunted by the souls of the anguished crew members of the ill-fated ship.

Three-masted schooner in the distance from Boon Island rocky shore.

Nearly 100 years before Boon Island Lighthouse was built, the British merchant ship *Nottingham Galley* set sail from England for Boston on a rainy day in September 25, 1710. In his log, Captain John Dean recorded that the vessel was loaded with special ropes and cheese and had endured a challenging and slow voyage hindered by storms and poor weather. Dean, who had previously worked as a butcher, made the transition to a life at sea and discovered that he greatly preferred his new role as a sailor, eventually achieving the rank of Captain.

On December 11, 1710, the *Nottingham Galley* was caught in a winter nor'easter, tossed about through sleet, snow, and heavy seas. The vessel crashed and sank off the exposed barren island known as Boon Island. At the time, all 14 men survived and made it to safety on the icy rock. The only items salvaged just before the wreck sank were small pieces of soggy cheese, part of a broken mast, fragments of a torn sail, and some canvas.

Shipwreck Etching by Harry Chase (c. 1870)
Image Library of Congress

That night, the men endured a freezing night of wind, sleet, and snow battering the island. They fashioned a triangular tent from the parts of the sail and canvas, which the men huddled in as closely as possible to conserve heat and avoid prolonged exposure to the elements.

By noon on the second day, the ship's cook died from exposure due to an illness he had contracted during the voyage. He received a sailor's Christian burial at sea. The crew's hands and feet were numb and beginning to fall victim to frostbite. They tried to remove their ice-covered boots and clothing which exposed their limbs to the cold while trying to dry their skin. They attempted to wrap their feet in pieces of canvas and rope fibers for protection.

The crew could see the main shore about six miles away, but there were no trees or means to start a fire on the desolate piece of rock to signal anyone ashore about their plight, or to provide warmth in the extreme winter conditions. For food, they finished the soggy cheese within days and then consumed the kelp and rockweed sparingly, rationing three mussels daily until the frozen supply ran out after less than a week. Once the food was gone, two crew members succumbed to exposure and starvation.

Realizing that no one on the distant shore could see them in the harsh winter weather, the men decided to build a makeshift raft to launch. The ship's carpenter was gravely ill and unable to assist. The men were now starving, as their meager rations of mussels and seaweed were not enough for survival. With the help of a determined crew member known only as the "Swede," they constructed a raft from whatever debris they could salvage from the wreckage. They selected two men, one of whom was the Swede, to take the raft and seek help. They launched the craft during high tide amidst the turbulent seas, with orders to light a fire on shore once they landed to signal their comrades on the island. As the raft approached within a few miles of the mainland, it overturned, and the two men drowned in the icy waters.

Waves crashing along rocky shore on cloudy day.

Days passed, and no sign of the raft making the shore was observed. Food was unavailable, except for some morsels of frozen seaweed, as their plight was now in its second week after the incident. The carpenter, a 47-year-old portly man, had perished from illness and exposure. The men, who were now driven to madness by starvation, came to the captain with a plea to eat the flesh of their comrade to survive. After much moral deliberation, Captain Dean decided to allow this horrific act to provide some nourishment for his men for a few more days, hoping that someone would find them soon before they all perished.

Dean knew what to do as a previously trained butcher before becoming the ship's captain. He first dehumanized the man by cutting off his head, hands, and feet and dressing the flesh. He proceeded to slice the flesh for the crew and dip it in the salt water. The men ate so ravenously that the captain became very concerned they would devour the corpse in one day. He and a few men moved the body and stored it safely away from the tent and the crew. He proceeded to deal out the ghoulish diet in small portions each day. The captain would later write of the change into irrational behavior of the men, as they became fierce and reckless and the most "pitiful objects of despair."

On January 2, more than three weeks after the wreck, remains of the makeshift raft appeared on the shore. The tide carried the body of one of the two men to the main beach, where local fishermen discovered it, while the body of the Swede was never found. The York County coroner, Lewis Bane, was called to examine the lifeless body frozen in a tangle of seaweed on the beach at Wells, Maine. He traveled to Cape Neddick, where he persuaded local fisherman John Stover to take him to Boon Island since no local fishermen were reported missing. He suspected that the body must have been a survivor from Boon Island after a shipwreck. With a crew of three, they boarded Stover's fishing shallop and headed out to sea. They spotted a flapping white tent-like structure with figures outside it waving their scraggy arms as they approached.

The starved and delirious crew saw the fishing boat approaching the island and mustered all the strength they could, waving their arms frantically. The seas were heavy, and the rescue crew could only bring the fishing boat within a few hundred yards of the survivors. They sent one man in a dory to provide supplies for building a fire. When he returned, the exhausted rescuer told his captain how shocked he was upon seeing the shipwrecked crew, saying he was frightened. He observed the skeletal captain, covered in sores and blood, which rendered him speechless, and the men in the tent were in even worse shape. Unable to bring the crew on board due to the high seas, they promised to help the next day. The next day arrived, but the waters were still too rough for a rescue. However, the captain would later write that they could at least build a fire to warm themselves and boil their "meat."

The survivors, resembling skeletons more than live individuals, were rescued on January 4, 1710, nearly four weeks after their shipwreck on Boon Island. They were taken to the fishing boat, two or three at a time, and were given bread and spirits, which made them violently ill as their bodies struggled to adjust from their previous horrific diet. When the ten survivors finally reached a tavern by the shore around 8 p.m., most were on the edge of death due to starvation and exposure, and had to be carried into the tavern. Many had hands and feet blackened by frostbite and had lost the use of parts of their limbs.

Rocky Coast of York, Maine, in Winter

Captain Deane wrote his relatively "harmless" report at the tavern, stating that they got caught in a storm and had to eat the carpenter crew member out of desperation. However, only three of his men signed it, while the others strongly objected to his numerous claims. They blamed him for the shipwreck, insisting he had cried and panicked when the ship ran aground and that he was the one who suggested cannibalism. The crew members noted that he had even attempted to deliver the vessel to French privateers to collect the insurance money.

The first mate, Christopher Langman, provided a conflicting account in his writing, which most of the crew agreed with and endorsed. He claimed that Captain Dean had deliberately planned to wreck the ship to collect insurance money for himself and his brother, who were the ship's primary owners. Other crew members corroborated his claim when they reported overhearing conversations between the captain and his brother. The first mate noted that the captain placed the crew on short rations and beat several dissenters to break the spirit of anyone opposing him as the *Nottingham Galley* crossed the Atlantic from England.

In his statement, Langman reported that the ship was circling in the Gulf of Maine, searching for more French privateers interested in buying the ship. The brothers had complete disregard for the crew, especially with a nor'easter approaching. He noted that he tried to convince Dean to steer further out to sea, but the captain put a pistol to his head and confined him to his bunk.

Langman returned to England to publish his side of the story but his health failed and he died shortly afterward, which many believe resulted from his body's grueling experience at Boon Island. Captain Dean survived the ordeal but left England in disgrace when newspapers got hold of the story, as the court sided with the first mate and most of the crew. The captain would spend the rest of his life trying to restore his good name.

Dean later enlisted as a mercenary in the Russian Navy, commanded a frigate, and was responsible for capturing over 20 enemy ships for the Russians. In his final venture, while in command of a Russian vessel, he captured two Swedish ships when an English and a Dutch man-of-war vessel appeared. They accused him of accepting bribes to hand over the Swedish ships to the English. A court-martial found him guilty, and he was demoted.

The resilient commander ultimately returned to England, became a spy, and persuaded his superiors that he had uncovered a conspiracy against the Crown. He married a wealthy woman and produced another history of Boon Island, republishing his account of the *Nottingham Galley* multiple times. In 1728, he received a diplomatic appointment. He retired comfortably and lived to an old age of 81, with many considering him a hero. His account of the events in Boon Island circulated worldwide for many years afterward.

Boon Island Lighthouse towering over rocky desolate island.

Although the *Nottingham Galley* incident occurred long before the current Boon Island Lighthouse was built on this desolate rock, the event created a demand for some type of light or warning device to assist mariners navigating around this small island. The government subsequently financed the construction of lighthouses along the coast during the latter part of the 1700s and well into the nineteenth century. Boon Island Light was erected in 1811 due to the numerous shipwrecks in the area.

Today, Boon Island Lighthouse stands as the tallest lighthouse in New England. In 1995, nine small iron cannons and other artifacts were discovered just off Boon Island in approximately 25 feet of water. It turned out that they were from the *Nottingham Galley* wreck.

Years later after the lighthouse was built, many of Boon Island's light keepers, who had served on this barren, isolated island, would often speak of its terrible solitude and the overwhelming loneliness surrounding the enclosed area. Many have reported hearing moaning or crying noises over the tiny island believed to be the tortured souls of either those that had perished on Boon Island, or those who participated in the gruesome act for their survival.

Keeper's Wife Loses Her Mind

Boon Island Light, York, Maine

Boon Island Lighthouse stands on a small, desolate rock island that measures about 400 square yards and rises barely 14 feet above sea level at its highest point. Located 6 miles from the main shoreline, it has been the site of numerous shipwrecks. Reports of a female ghost at Boon Island have persisted for many years. Some believe she may be one of the wives of the men from the *Nottingham Galley*, which wrecked on the island in 1710, even though there were no women aboard the ship at the time of the wreck; or from one of the many other shipwrecks that occurred around the island.

Many believe that the ghost haunting the area is the distraught wife of a former keeper named Lucas Bright. Her husband drowned on Boon Island during a gale storm. However, no records of a keeper named Lucas Bright at Boon Island Light exist, which may place this story in the realm of folklore. Some argue that he might have been intentionally left out of the records due to his brief service on the island, lasting only a few months, to avoid any scandal at the time. Nonetheless, the story remains intriguing, as it explains the known presence of a female spirit on the island, witnessed by many respected keepers and caretakers.

This tragic tale highlights the physical and emotional dangers that many lighthouse keepers and their wives faced while stationed at a remote lighthouse. The position may have seemed exciting to many young brides of keepers in the 1800s, but it quickly became a source of emotional stress, with a beacon located miles away from the mainland. There have been numerous accounts of keepers who lost their lives in their roles at lighthouse stations due to tragic accidents resulting from storms, illnesses, or from the deplorable conditions of the structures.

Highest tower in New England.

97

The story goes that in the mid-1800s, First Assistant Lucas Bright arrived at Boon Island Lighthouse with his new bride, Katherine. A few months after they settled on the small, desolate rock, gale-force winds from a severe December nor'easter swept across the tiny island, hurling massive waves over its rocky surface.

Lucus Bright had been feeling unwell for the past week and was physically drained, but he needed to check the tower to ensure the lantern was lit for any mariners caught in the winter storm, so they could find safety near the shore. He tied a rope around his waist and kissed his wife before leaving the warm house, stepping into the biting winds and spray as he headed toward the tower. Waves crashed all around him, coating the rocks with sheets of ice while he tried to secure a bolt to the tower's door. Suddenly, a massive rogue wave swept over the rocks and engulfed the keeper. He lost his grip, slipped on the icy terrain, and fell into the freezing waters, drowning.

Katherine watched the accident in horror and managed to grasp the rope tied to her husband, preventing him from drifting away. She ventured into the storm and somehow pulled her husband's body ashore, then dragged him over the slippery rocks into the lighthouse tower, leaving him at the bottom of the stairs. Overwhelmed with grief and shock, she sat beside him and held his hand for as long as she could endure.

Vintage Image Boon Island Light
Courtesy US Coast Guard

The storm raged on, and Katherine knew she had to tend to the light so that others would not meet the same fate as her beloved. For five days and nights during this seemingly endless tempest, Katherine, consumed by grief, took on all the responsibilities of the lighthouse. She ate the little food that remained and slept very little. Carrying heavy buckets of kerosene, she climbed the 168 stairs of New England's tallest lighthouse each day, braving freezing temperatures to keep the lamp working and protect any mariners from the relentless storms and heaving waves. Afterward, she would stay close to her husband's frozen body, sometimes holding his hand or hugging him while speaking to him as if to comfort herself.

On the sixth day after the storms had finally passed, Katherine was nearly out of fuel and too exhausted and tormented to light the beacon, causing the light to go out. The tower was freezing cold from days of the violent storm. She slipped into a deep sleep from the devastating experience.

Once the light had gone out and the seas had calmed, fishermen from York went to the lighthouse to investigate. They found no one in the house and proceeded to the tower. The temperature inside the tower had dropped to a freezing ten degrees below zero. There they discovered Katherine Bright, freezing from exposure and driven to madness by grief and exhaustion. She was sitting at the bottom of the stairs, holding the frozen corpse of her husband. The fishermen managed to bring Katherine and her husband's body ashore, but by that time, she had completely lost her mind. She died shortly thereafter.

Although this story has become part of Maine folklore, there appears to be a helpful female spirit on the island that is still dealing with a traumatic event from her life. Over the years, many mariners and keepers have reported seeing a ghostly figure of a young, sad-faced woman shrouded in white on the rocks at dusk. Occasionally, sounds of moaning and crying have also been heard. On some nights, lighthouse keepers have mentioned hearing knocking on the door, and when they open it, they see a faint apparition of a woman dressed in white heading toward the tower. Sometimes, a keeper would bring their cat or dog to Boon Island, but most of these animals would refuse to enter the lighthouse tower. Sometimes dogs would be spotted chasing something around the rocks, barking nonstop as if to warn the phantom intruder.

One Coast Guardsman became a believer in the ghost stories in the early 1970s when he and a fellow crewman were fishing off the small rocky island and drifted too far out to return in time to turn on the light before dark. No one was on the island, yet somehow the light was shining brightly when they returned. Others have claimed to have heard doors mysteriously opening and closing, or feeling like someone was watching when they performed their duties at the lighthouse.

Ghost Stays on to Help His Friend

Goat Island (Cape Porpoise) Light, York, Maine

Goat Island Light, also known as Cape Porpoise Lighthouse, was constructed in 1835 to guide mariners into Cape Porpoise Harbor, which had become a bustling fishing center. There are perilous inlets, ledges, and sharp rocks in many areas surrounding Goat Island, which continued to claim ships, even with the lighthouse nearby. The island lies about a mile offshore, and between 1865 and 1920, nearly 50 vessels wrecked near the island. Fortunately, there were no fatalities from these accidents, thanks to the bravery of the keepers at Goat Island.

Various families have taken care of the property for many years. Scott Dombrowski and his family have been the main caretakers for over 30 years. They have hosted scouting troops and college classes and have served as tour guides for over 2,000 summer visitors to the lighthouse each year. Other families also assist in sharing responsibilities throughout the year, especially during the winter months. They are all considered the last resident lighthouse-keeping families in Maine.

Scott Dombrowski lost his best friend Dick Curtis to the island's treacherous storms many years ago. However, Curtis, even in death, remains at the residence and island, hanging out with his lifelong friend.

Goat Island (Cape Porpoise) Lighthouse at low tide.

Scott Dombrowski and Dick Curtis had been friends since childhood; both grew up in Marblehead, Massachusetts, joined the Coast Guard, and later moved to the Cape Porpoise area near Goat Island Light for employment at the station. Curtis began his role as the main caretaker on Goat Island in 1994, becoming well-known for his sense of humor. He was single and lived with his dogs. The two friends often joked that if either of them passed away, they would remain to haunt the lighthouse because of their love for the area and its residents.

In 2002, on a sunny Memorial Day, Dick Curtis was on shore in Cape Porpoise by the harbor master's building. He took care of two dogs for a friend and had two of his own, so he decided to take all four animals on a boat ride in the early evening. He returned to the lighthouse to pick up the dogs and set off to enjoy the sunset.

The next day, those on the shore realized that Curtis had not returned the previous evening, as he had only intended to go out for the sunset and return with the dogs. A search party was sent out, and after several hours, they found his boat overturned at the far corner of Goat Island, facing the ocean. His body was eventually discovered, indicating that he had drowned. Two of the dogs he brought with him made it to shore and were later found, but the other two were missing.

Dombrowski became the main caretaker of the island after his friend's death. Later that summer, during a tour around the island, he overheard one of the women on the tour, who happened to be a psychic, tell her companion, "This place is haunted." When he asked her later what she meant, she explained that Dick Curtis was there with a message for him, assuring him that he was all right and would be staying at the lighthouse. When the tour concluded and the guests were waiting at the boat launch to be taken back to shore, the psychic began to chant repeatedly, "One of the dogs made it."

Throughout that summer and fall, Dombrowski noticed that Curtis made his presence felt. A vent fan was suddenly activated in front of a room full of guests, and lost items consistently reappeared on the kitchen table. Other incidents included the foghorn sounding off even in broad daylight and continuing to blare even when turned off. He believed that the spirit of his friend used this as a way of communicating with him.

Goat Island (Cape Porpoise) Lighthouse lies about a mile from the shore.

The presidential Bush family owned a summer home in Kennebunkport, near the lighthouse at Walker's Point, and were often seen there as former President George H. W. Bush Sr. and his wife, Barbara, visited the shops. They were always seen stopping for ice cream and socializing with the residents. They were beloved by the community, and secret service agents would frequent Goat Island to keep a watchful eye on the area during their visits.

That fall, following the death of Dick Curtis, former President George Bush Sr. returned to the area with his wife, accompanied by the Secret Service to ensure safety. A series of boats patrolled the waters as the former president ventured out in their boat past the lighthouse. Dombrowski remarked to his friend about what a fun spectacle it was to see the former President visiting nearby, and the foghorn sounded off as if in response, much to his amazement.

Dombrowski would greet his new friendly spirit every time he landed by the lighthouse, and often, when he reached a certain spot on the beach, the foghorn would sound once as if in response. Due to the sporadic occurrences of the foghorn, the Coast Guard replaced the entire unit.

One cold day, Dombrowski sat in front of an old electric heater that hadn't worked for years and asked his Curtis' spirit for warmth. Suddenly, the heater turned on. Reports of a faint apparition have been seen in the keeper's house window, and the island sometimes is wrapped in fog on otherwise clear days, indicating Dick Curtis is planning to stay and help at the lighthouse.

Ghosts Around Wood Island

Wood Island Light, Biddeford, Maine

Wood Island Lighthouse was constructed in 1808, marking the entrance to the Saco River, about a couple miles from the Biddeford mainland and about a mile from the Biddeford Pool peninsula. However, it faced ongoing issues due to its poor construction. It is Maine's second-oldest lighthouse, after Portland Head Light. The island was covered in trees until 1869 when they were destroyed by a fierce winter gale and later by fire that same year. The lighthouse was rebuilt in 1858 as the beacon and the island have become the source of legends, rescues, and ghost stories over the years.

One of the most famous Maine lighthouse stories revolves around an actual tragedy-suicide that occurred on the island near Wood Island Lighthouse. Their ghosts have reportedly haunted the island ever since, among others.

Wood Island Lighthouse lies on the edge of the rocky shore.

Frederick Milliken served as a game warden and part-time officer at Biddeford Pool, a rural community on a peninsula adjacent to the city of Biddeford, Maine. He resided on Wood Island with his wife and three stepchildren, and he was a large, gentle man in his late thirties, known as the town's "gentle giant." His wife was previously married to Warren Rich, who had died from injuries suffered when his hip was crushed while on his ship and had been crippled for several years. Milliken owned a house along with a small shack located a few hundred yards away on the southern part of the island. That shack had once been used for raising chickens. Keeper Thomas Orcutt lived near the Millikens at Wood Island Light.

Two drifters in their mid-twenties, Howard "Wiley" Hobbs and William Moses, persuaded Milliken to rent them his vacant shack for a brief stay. They cooked on the bottom floor, and a wooden step ladder led up to the loft, where they slept on an old couch or the floor. Both young men had serious drinking problems and, over the following months, did not pay their rent to Milliken.

On Sunday, May 31, 1896, both Hobbs and Moses went on a drinking binge in the nearby town of Old Orchard and were kicked out for being drunk and disorderly by the deputy sheriff there. On Monday morning, they went over to Camp Ellis Pier and then headed to Hill's Beach to continue drinking before taking their boat back to Wood Island

On Monday afternoon, June 1, Milliken was at the boat landing with one of his sons when they saw both drunken men coming to land their boat. Milliken told them to meet him at his house to discuss their overdue rent. They agreed, and both men went back to the shanty. Hobbs picked up his hunting rifle, and Moses asked him why he needed the gun, telling him he should leave it at home. His friend replied that he might find some birds to shoot.

At around 4:30 that afternoon, Hobbs and Moses met Milliken outside his garden, next to his house, where the officer had put on his badge to discuss the rent. Milliken, noticing the rifle, asked if it was loaded, to which Hobbs replied that it wasn't. Worried about his safety and that of the people in his house with Hobbs holding a gun while intoxicated, he said, "I'll see whether it is or not." As he reached for the gun, Hobbs backed away and, almost instinctively believing he was in danger, placed the weapon on his shoulder and fired. The bullet lodged itself in the upper right side of Milliken's abdomen. His wife watched the incident in horror but kept calm and ran out of the house to help bring her wounded husband back inside, with the assistance of William Moses. Hobbs followed, apologizing while still holding the rifle.

They laid Milliken on the bed. Realizing he was in critical condition, she asked Moses to quickly row back to the mainland with one of her sons to get immediate medical assistance. Hobbs then asked if there was anything he could do to help, and she replied that he could take off her husband's shoes.

As he removed his shoes, he blamed the victim for his predicament. His wife pleaded with him to give her the gun, but he threatened to use it on her if she attempted to take it from him. Milliken, listening to the conversation while experiencing immense pain, calmly asked his attacker not to hurt his wife, to which Hobbs replied that he wouldn't, as he still held the rifle. To diminish the situation, she told Hobbs to go to the lighthouse and inform Keeper Thomas Orcutt of what had occurred.

Still, in a drunken daze, Hobbs stumbled over to the keeper's dwelling, seeking help from Keeper Orcutt while still carrying the rifle. Orcutt, seeing the gun, would not let Hobbs inside but met him outside his house and tried his best to calm the guilty man. Hobbs briefly explained what had happened, still blaming Milliken for his behavior. The keeper ran to the crime scene to help, leaving Hobbs walking behind, but he was too late to provide any assistance. Frederick Milliken had died from his wounds less than an hour after being shot.

Boardwalk or wooden walkway to Wood Island Light.

Hobbs trailed at a distance behind Orcutt, still holding his rifle. Upon reaching the house, he asked about Milliken's condition and was told that the officer had died. Orcutt urged the attacker to surrender to the authorities. However, Hobbs, realizing he might spend the rest of his life in jail, declared that he had one bullet left, which he intended to use on himself. He dashed back to his shack, with no one following him for fear of their own safety. He penned a brief note to his friend William Moses and another to a girl he had been seeing in Biddeford, saying goodbye. He then climbed up to the loft and shot himself in the head.

Moses and one of the Milliken's children arrived with a doctor around 6:30 p.m., but they were too late, as the gentle giant had passed away. He went to the shack, where he found his friend in a pool of blood. When questioned later, he and Milliken's wife gave the deputy the same statements, confirming that there was no animosity between the assailant and the victim.

Jagged rocks by tower of Wood Island Lighthouse.

Since the incident, numerous strange occurrences have been reported at Wood Island. Many believe that the spirits of Hobbs and Milliken haunt the vicinity of Wood Island Lighthouse. Moans were still heard from the shack until it was finally removed, and locked doors mysteriously opened at the lighthouse. Dark shadows have been spotted near the walkway and at the top of the tower. Footsteps have been heard ascending into the tower, along with unusual voices.

There have also been sightings of a woman believed to be Milliken's wife. She is a faint apparition seen around the keeper's house and nearby grounds.

In 1905, a fisherman living alone on the island became so distressed by the belief that he was seeing and hearing ghosts that he stayed overnight in a boarding house on the mainland in Saco. The next day, he jumped from a third-floor window to his death.

Investigators Find Many Spirits

The New England Ghost Project, led by Ron Kolek and four other members, including a psychic medium named Maureen Wood, were invited to investigate the island and lighthouse area. They set up specialized equipment, including infrared cameras and EVP devices for audio recording to filter out background noise. They observed and recorded shadowy figures near the lighthouse and walkway. A spirit, believed to be Hobbs, communicated through Maureen's trance, expressing regret while they were at the top of the lighthouse tower. She also heard a sobbing female voice thought to belong to Milliken's wife. Outside on the ground, another spirit, believed to be Frederick Milliken himself, caused Maureen to collapse to her knees, making her feel as if she were severely injured and trying to escape.

The team members only knew that there had been a tragic murder-suicide on the island and were intentionally not given any details to remain unbiased. They decided to move their equipment to the attic of the keeper's house. They saw bright green lights drifting in the darkness and then asked Maureen to come up to see if they could make contact, but no communication was made.

The group went out to the boardwalk as Maureen described seeing black shadows swooping in front of her. They moved to the basement of the keeper's house, where she contacted possibly the same male spirit of Hobbs, who again expressed remorse. Then, a female spirit made herself known through the medium. This time, the infrared camera captured an image. When the photos were later developed, the series showed an initial orb that transformed into a human female form. Could it be Milliken's wife?

The team returned to the tower on another visit and discovered a male spirit, not a keeper, who may have either fallen down the stairs or had been pushed and died from a head injury.

Another trip with some members of the earlier team followed. Ron Kolek received a call from a man in Missouri who had a vivid dream about three girls murdered not simultaneously but sequentially over a span of time near Wood Island Light. The team had already been planning this trip, which presented an intriguing reason to return once more. As in previous excursions, he made sure that Maureen Wood, the medium, and other team members remained unaware of any specific details.

The team began work after dark and continued until well past 2 a.m., as this was the time when most hauntings occur. They set up a safe area and followed Maureen out to the boardwalk, where she used a special dowsing technique, holding a piece of citron hanging from a chain and observing the direction in which it swung to indicate where spirits were present. She discovered a female spirit and started asking questions. The team learned that the spirit had been murdered on the island and was lost, and that an "Indian" had killed her. The spirit was searching for help.

Maureen then led the team through the darkness to the northern part of the island, just off the wooden boardwalk, where another spirit revealed that more than three girls were buried at the site and that a shack once stood there. The spirit informed her that they had been killed one by one and that the shack had been set on fire afterward, which closely aligned with the vivid dream the man in Missouri had shared only with Ron Kolek. "The people who died here were trapped on the island and held against their will," said the medium. "They say they want their story to be told."

The team decided to return to the basement of the keeper's building where they had previously encountered a female spirit, whom they believed might have been Milliken's wife. However, the entity was uncooperative, as Maureen sensed her anger over the team trying to photograph her the previous year, and she made no effort to communicate afterward. The group chose to leave the spirit alone, but Ron wanted to set up an infrared camera in the basement room with candles lit. He unscrewed the light bulbs, and as they went upstairs, the lights turned back on. The spirit in the basement had indicated that it wanted no involvement with the team.

Based on the activity recorded from observing green lights during their previous visit, the team decided to return to the attic of the keeper's house.

Maureen asked everyone to hold hands as she tried communicating with any spirits present. The sound of pouring rain was audible, and then it abruptly stopped. Her grip tightened around her teammates as her voice deepened, taking on the tone of a man with a Spanish accent. The spirit she was channeling claimed he had been on the island for nearly a year before he died. He introduced himself as Roger and stated that the year was 1762. He was furious because his captain had deserted him and his shipmates on the island. He explained that there had been ten of them at the start, and he was one of three left. When asked what flag he sailed under, the spirit replied, "I fly under no flag." Ron Polek responded, "If you fly under no flag, that must mean you're a pirate." The spirit warned him to be very careful of his accusation.

The angry spirit began to repeatedly express how cold it felt. The medium's hand grew colder as she spoke, and her grip tightened on her frightened teammates. Her body temperature was also dropping. Ron demanded that the spirit leave. At first, it refused, but eventually, it departed. The team decided to call it a night, but Maureen mentioned that she could still hear voices coming from upstairs in the keeper's house (no one was upstairs), and some old folk-style music was playing.

View of Wood Island from the lighthouse tower.

Spirits Around Cape Elizabeth

Cape Elizabeth Light (Two Lights), Cape Elizabeth, Maine

Constructed in 1829, the Cape Elizabeth Twin Lights consisted of two range light towers, commonly referred to as "Two Lights." During a fierce blizzard in January 1885, one of the greatest rescues by any lighthouse keeper was performed by Keeper Marcus Hanna. Despite suffering from the flu, upon seeing the ship *Australia* in distress offshore, he crawled over snowdrifts and then waded into the freezing ocean waters up to his waist. He was able to get a line to the wreck and carefully drag two barely surviving crew members ashore, putting his own life in great danger. Hanna received a rare gold lifesaving medal for his extraordinary bravery and determination to save those men.

The west tower was dismantled in 1924, and only the east tower continues to operate today, now known as Cape Elizabeth Light. There are reports of hauntings around the lighthouse and nearby. They involve the spirit of a previous keeper, cries of help on the nearby shoreline from a shipwreck, and sightings of the "Ghost Bride of Crescent Beach."

Cape Elizabeth Lighthouse at twilight.

Dedicated Keeper Remains On Duty

Joseph H. Upton, like his father, was a ship captain. However, prior to that, he mainly served as a ferry steamboat captain for nearly 15 years, starting at the age of 18 by transporting passengers throughout Casco Bay in Portland. When a local fire station in South Portland was established in 1892, the young man volunteered as one of its charter members. He also served as company captain from 1909 to 1910.

In 1893, his older brothers George and Horace were caught in a severe storm aboard the fishing schooner *Mary Lizzie*. His brother Horace perished with five other crew members as the vessel sank. His other brother George barely survived after drifting in the waters for nearly a day and a half.

Joseph had always been passionate about lighthouses and decided to change careers to enter the lighthouse service. He climbed the ranks from an assistant keeper at remote Matinicus Rock Light in 1911 to various roles at light stations along the coast, including White Island Light in New Hampshire (Isles of Shoals). In 1926, he finally achieved his dream of becoming the keeper at Cape Elizabeth Light, cherishing its proximity to the rugged shoreline and the warm local community.

On a chilly Saturday evening in January 1934, a winter storm caused the main lights to fail, resulting in a minor issue with the auxiliary light. The 65-year-old lighthouse keeper left his warm bed around 9:30 p.m. to adjust the auxiliary light in the tower, ensuring that the lantern flashed correctly on the east tower of Cape Elizabeth Light despite the storm. His wife, Mabel, was asleep and unaware of his absence.

Around 11:30 p.m., she woke up and noticed her husband was missing; she called the tower room but got no response. Worried, she ventured out in the freezing cold to the tower and found him unconscious at the bottom of the stairs. It appeared he had slipped and fallen while trying to adjust the light at the top. She called a doctor, but Upton had sustained multiple skull fractures, and his injuries were too severe for recovery. He passed away hours later, around 5:30 a.m. on Sunday, January 14, just before dawn.

There have been claims of an apparition of an elderly man in a lighthouse uniform from that era near the tower or driveway, believed to be Upton's spirit. Footsteps leading up to the tower have also been heard and tools have been rearranged.

Cries From Shipwrecked Victims of the *Bohemian*

On February 4, 1864, the 295-foot steamship *Bohemian* was on a winter voyage from Liverpool, England, to Portland, Maine. The ship was carrying about 219 passengers, including 200 Irish immigrants and 19 cabin-class passengers. The *Bohemian* was only a couple of miles from the rocky shoreline of Cape Elizabeth and dangerously close to Alden's Rock, a perilous ledge in shallow water that was marked at the time only by a silent buoy, not by a bell buoy. Captain Borland miscalculated the distance in the dense, foggy conditions.

By 8 o'clock, the first officer had just taken the wheel when the buoy marking the dangerous rock was spotted directly ahead. The captain yelled to shut off the engines to slow the vessel, but it was too late. The *Bohemian* struck Alden's Rock, tearing a gash in the hull. Borland tried to steer the vessel toward shore, eventually reaching an inlet about two miles from the mainland. Still, the disabled steamer could not proceed any further under power due to the water it had taken on and the damage in the engine room. The steamer could only drift toward shore. The captain ordered the gunboats to fire to signal the ship's distress, but only one could be fired as the other was already underwater. The captain of a pilot boat was a mile away and heard the single gunshot, but mistakenly believed the ship was celebrating President's Day.

Most lifeboats launched during the hysteria weren't filled and mainly contained men. The terrified passengers and crew on the lifeboats initially refused to return to the sinking ship to rescue those stranded on the deck, fearing they might capsize. Some of those left on the wreck jumped overboard, hoping to be pulled into the boats, but many drowned from exposure while struggling in the freezing winter waters.

With the lifeboats dispatched, Captain Borland, four crew members, and about seventy passengers found themselves stranded on deck. With the steamer's bridge completely submerged and waves crashing over it, Borland realized that the time for the ship to remain afloat was running out. The steamer was less than two miles from shore when some of the passengers noticed that a couple of lifeboats were returning to assist in the rescue efforts. Additional help was also coming from shore residents who heard about the ship's distress, with some sending teams risking their lives to aid the survivors.

112

Some of those stranded, many of whom were women and children, who were still waiting and unable to climb up the masts and rigging, were washed overboard as the ship began to sink into the icy waters. Captain Borland managed to get about fifty passengers and most of his crew safely off the wreck. He and his remaining crew waited until all the survivors were in the lifeboats before they climbed into the last lifeboat heading to shore. An hour and a half later, the *Bohemian* sank.

"Shipwreck at Night" painting of the *Bohemian* wreck by Alzira Peirce (1939).

In total, two crew members and forty passengers, all Irish immigrants from the lower steerage class, lost their lives. The residents of Cape Elizabeth opened their homes, providing food, shelter, and clothing to the exhausted survivors, while the local City Hall served as a temporary shelter for the next few days as survivors sought to notify their families in England and Ireland. The Portland Board of Trade collected money and distributed it to the survivors.

At the deposition, the jury determined that Captain Borland exercised poor judgment and was responsible for the disaster, while his crew did not act professionally in assisting the passengers with the lifeboats, being more concerned with their own safety. Additionally, the captain of the pilot boat, who had heard the gun signaling the *Bohemian's* distress but chose not to intervene, was also deemed at fault.

Days later, some women from nearby Cape Elizabeth found items from the *Bohemian* wreck washed up in the beach, including bolts of wool, silks, and satins, which many used to create new clothing for the harsh winter. At least twelve of the 42 lives lost are commemorated by a small monument in nearby Calvary Cemetery in South Portland.

Over the years their have been reports of sounds of cries for help being heard along the shore and over the winter waters late at night, believed to be from the passengers who perished on the *Bohemian*.

The Lady in White, or the Ghost Bride of Crescent Beach

This female spirit often visits Crescent Beach, where she was found after a shipwreck a short distance from Cape Elizabeth Light. She also haunts the Inn by the Sea, where she was laid to rest behind the beach.

On July 12, 1807, Lydia Carver, who was 23 years old and the daughter of a Portland businessman named Amos Carver, was engaged to a local man. Along with most of her bridal party, she traveled on the schooner *Charles* to Boston to find her perfect wedding dress. After spending time exploring shops, she finally found the ideal dress that suited her style. Carver boarded the same schooner in Boston Harbor, accompanied by 21 other passengers, most of whom were her wedding entourage, sailing back to Portland.

A gale swept in that evening, creating heavy seas as the schooner navigated up the coast. Just before midnight, the ship entered a thick fog near Cape Elizabeth Light and crashed onto a rocky ledge called Watts Ledge just offshore. Upon running onto the ledge, everyone's worst nightmare would come true. The vessel then turned broadside to the waves, which battered it against the rocks throughout the night. The schooner tipped onto its side as the rocks tore a gaping hole in the bottom of the hull. For nearly 12 hours, no rescue attempts could be made from shore due to the storm's ferocity, as massive waves continued to slam against the helpless ship.

Realizing that chances for rescue would not happen until the storm subsided, some passengers tried to secure themselves to the rigging and wait for help as the waves continued to crash over the ship. Captain Adams of the schooner knew they were a short distance from Richmond Island as he and three other men attempted to swim there to signal for help. His wife called out in anguish for him to return to the ship, but the turbulent seas were too much for the captain and the other men as they were swept away and pulled under the waves.

As the storm raged on during the night, the seas began to cause the ship to break apart. Those who attached themselves to the rigging or tied themselves to parts of the boat met their deaths when the ship began to flip over and sink into the treacherous waters. The dense fog blanketing the area that evening led to further confusion after the vessel broke up, causing others to perish amongst the waves trying to make it to shore.

By morning, the storm had finally passed, but nearby Crescent Beach was strewn with debris from the wrecked ship. Bodies began to wash ashore, as sixteen people lost their lives that day. Among those found near the beach were the bodies of Captain Adams and his wife. Lydia Carver was also not one of the six survivors that day; her body was also discovered on the beach, holding onto the trunk containing the special wedding dress she had purchased. She was buried in a graveyard behind the Inn by the Sea, a short distance from the beach where she was found.

Schooner sailing ships passing by one another.

Carver's ghost, always dressed in white, is said to linger around the inn and stroll the nearby beach. Many believe that spirits from tragic accidents may linger in the area where they perished. She has been observed, especially in foggy weather and on the anniversary of her death each year, walking along the shore of Crescent Beach dressed in white, as if in search of her husband to be. Footprints on Crescent Beach have been found with no beginning or end, as if her spirit wandered back and forth, shaken by an unfulfilled dream. She is observed as sad-faced and has been named as the "Ghost Bride of Crescent Beach."

The Inn by the Sea is behind Crescent Beach, just a short distance from Cape Elizabeth Light. Her ghost is often seen dressed in white, seemingly preparing for her wedding and enjoying the company at the inn. Staff members report witnessing the elevator moving up and down by itself late at night, with the door opening and closing, though no one exits. When the elevator was empty, they would greet her ghost warmly, as they did not feel threatened. Visitors have reported smoke detectors going off in vacant rooms, only to fall silent minutes later. Her orb has been spotted drifting through walls from one room to another, and guests and staff members have seen a faint apparition in mirrors on some rooms.

One mother heard her children speaking to someone in an adjacent room, but no one was there when she entered. When she asked whom they were talking to, the kids pointed to the bed and said a lady had been sitting there. As the mother glanced at the bed, she noticed an imprint as if an adult had been sitting on it where no one had been before. At the restaurant inside the hotel, it was reported that place settings and dishes had been moved around.

Beachcombers have said that a strange fog will roll in over Richmond Island and you can see the masts of a wrecked ship sticking out of the fog. Some visitors to the beach have reported that on some evenings you can hear a tremendous crash followed by screams echoing from the Watts Ledge area.

One traveler driving in her car near the beach noticed a young woman in a wedding gown next to a deer standing by the side of the road. When she made eye contact, a few seconds later the faint apparition vanished and the deer ran into the woods.

Although nearly 220 years old, Lydia Carver's 5-foot gravestone is in remarkable condition compared to those around it. Even the detailed engraving above the type shows little signs of wear over the last two centuries. The inscription is still easy to read and remains with most of its initial detail. Perhaps Lydia's spirit is also taking care of her resting place.

Gravestone of Lydia Carver nearly 220 years old.

Portland Head Light Ghosts

Portland Head Light, Cape Elizabeth, Maine

One of the country's most famous and picturesque lighthouses, Portland Head Light, is the oldest in Maine, commissioned for construction by George Washington in 1791. Portland was one of the busiest shipping ports, as the beacon marked the entrance to Portland Harbor, facing Casco Bay. The lighthouse is situated within the 90-acre Fort Williams State Park. Fort Williams was built before the Spanish-American War in 1891 but was never used. The fort and its associated buildings became an active housing and training ground for troops, serving as a command post and headquarters during the early to mid-1900s. Occasionally, there have been sightings of ghostly soldiers dressed in World War I uniforms late at night. The spirits move about the fort and the surrounding grounds.

Massive wave breaks near Portland Head Lighthouse.

In 1876, two carriage drivers took a group of visitors to the lighthouse for the day and waited for their return. A storm out at sea had created huge swells, generating enormous waves during high tide that began crashing against the rocks where the drivers were stationed. Both drivers left their carriages and stood near the edge of the rocky shore, gazing at the breaking waves on the coast. Suddenly, a massive rogue wave swept over them, carrying both startled men out to sea. The next day, their bodies were found some distance away from the lighthouse. Their spirits have been seen wandering by the lighthouse.

Portland Head Lighthouse is said to also harbor the spirits of two longtime keepers of the light. One of the early keepers, Barzillai Delano was the third keeper assigned to the lighthouse. He was initially a blacksmith by trade and served from 1796 to 1820.

Joshua Strout, the more well-known of the keepers, maintained the lighthouse from 1869 to 1904. He was part of a family line that spanned four generations covering nearly 100 years of service. Strout was a sea captain of the ship *Andres* before a severe fall from the mast forced him to remain on shore. In 1869, he was made keeper of the Portland Head Light. He rarely took time away from the light and had gone nearly 17 years without taking any time off, retiring as Maine's oldest lighthouse keeper in 1904 at the age of 79.

The keeper frequently met with famous poet Henry Wadsworth Longfellow, who lived nearby in Portland. Longfellow's famous poem, "The Lighthouse," was believed to have been written while sitting on the rocks by Portland Head Light.

The most famous rescue of Strout and his family involves the wreck of the *Annie C. Maguire* on Christmas Eve in 1886, around 11:30 p.m. The vessel ran aground on the rocks less than 100 feet from Portland Head Lighthouse. The captain could not see the lighthouse in the heavy rains or possible snow squalls and misjudged his location. The Strouts rescued all eighteen people safely while the ship lay wedged on the rocks and remained as gracious as they could while the starving crew ate all their food. Creditors quickly seized the wreck later, but little was found of value. The captain and his wife, released days earlier, got away with stealing cash inside his wife's hat with other valuables.

Since the deaths of both keepers, numerous reports have emerged of footsteps believed to belong to one or both keepers climbing the tower stairs presumably to check on the light. Some previous keepers, staff members, and visitors have claimed to have seen faint apparitions in the tower and have felt cold spots in the upstairs of the keeper's building late in the evening.

118

Spirits of Seguin Island Light

Seguin Island Light, Georgetown, Maine

Seguin Island Lighthouse is the second oldest lighthouse in Maine. George Washington commissioned the construction of the first wooden tower in 1795, which stood for about 25 years. It is the highest lighthouse in Maine, perched on a rugged island with its lantern standing over 186 feet above sea level. The island is approximately two miles from the mouth of the Kennebec River and slightly further from the shore. The lighthouse was built to support the growing shipping and shipbuilding traffic along the Kennebec River and the seacoast. It features one of the largest foghorns, operating for nearly one-third of the year on many foggy days on the island. This lighthouse is among the few on the East Coast that still retains its original first-order Fresnel lens.

The history of Seguin Island Lighthouse is filled with strange, documented stories. It is considered the most haunted lighthouse in Maine and, arguably, New England. It is famous for the paranormal activity involving at least three different spirits or events frequently witnessed by many keepers, tourists, and mariners alike. These include mariners hearing a piano playing over the waters, the spirit of the first keeper, and a young girl buried on the island.

Seguin Island Light is the highest lighthouse in Maine, and the most haunted.

The Old Captain

The first keeper of Seguin Island Light was Major (Count) John Polereczky, a member of a noble Hungarian family with a rich heritage. Born in France, he fought alongside French troops during the American Revolution. Later, he settled in Dresden, Maine, where he served as the town clerk for 25 years before applying for and receiving the keeper position of Seguin Island Light in 1796. His modest salary made it challenging to live on the island, given its harsh and remote setting, and he frequently requested raises, all of which were denied. His brother-in-law, Christopher Pushard, served as his assistant and briefly brought his wife to the island, where they welcomed their first child, Jane. Unfortunately, Pushard's family didn't stay long because tensions grew between the two men.

After eight years of service, Polereczky died penniless on the island in 1804. For years afterward, some claim that his ghost has haunted the keepers who followed him. His apparition has been seen climbing the tower's staircase.

One incident occurred as the light station was being prepared for automation in 1985, the warrant officer in charge of the activities experienced an encounter with the ghost of the "old captain." The entity had awakened him in the middle of the night, dressed in oilskins and shaking his bed. The spirit asked him to leave the furniture and not disturb his home. Believing he was merely having a vivid dream, he ignored the captain's plea and proceeded to move the furniture, as he and his crew were required. The next

Seguin Island Light with its original first order Fresnel lens.

day, the furniture was loaded onto the dory, which sat on a skid on a track leading to the water. An order was given to start the engine, which would slowly lower the packed dory down to the ocean 200 feet below. The engine suddenly stopped dead, and the chain holding the dory broke, causing the overloaded boat to race down the track at full speed, hit the ocean waters, and sink on impact, taking the furniture with it.

In recent years, many dedicated volunteer caretakers who have committed to maintaining the lighthouse for summer tourists have reported various sightings and unusual paranormal occurrences. Items have been moved inside the house or thrown from shelves to the floor; mysterious cold spots have appeared; tools have vanished and reappeared randomly; and doors have been observed opening and closing by themselves. When the caretakers rearrange the furniture, they sometimes find it back in its original position the next day. Some claim to hear coughing from an unseen source. An apparition of an old sea captain has been sighted many times climbing the narrow, winding, iron spiral stairway leading to the top of the tower. Many believe these events are linked to the "Old Captain."

Piano Playing Causes Keeper's Insanity

According to the legend, around the mid-1800s, a caretaker or keeper of the beacon, recently married, took his young wife with him to tend to the light. Unaccustomed to the island's isolation, she grew increasingly bored and depressed, constantly complaining about having nothing to do. Believing it would occupy her mind and alleviate her boredom, the keeper arranged for a piano to be brought to the island just before winter set in. He proudly presented it to her after many attempts to maneuver the piano up the rocky ledge and carefully haul it to the keeper's house with the help of several friends.

His wife was thrilled but couldn't play without sheet music. Luckily, only one song came with the piano, so she started playing it. It was a simple Scott Joplin tune. Soon after, the island became icebound in winter's grasp, and no other deliveries could arrive. She continued to play her piano, repeating the same song over and over again.

The isolation and constant playing of the same tune for days into months eventually drove the keeper insane. Finally, he had enough, took an axe, and chopped up the piano, then turned on his complaining wife and killed her. Realizing the ghoulish action he just completed, he killed himself.

Many mariners and visitors to the island have reported hearing an old Scott Joplin tune played on a piano across the waters, especially during foggy weather. However, there is no record of any keeper murdering his wife, which places the story more in the realm of folklore. Some fishermen believe the event did not occur on Seguin Island, but that a murder by axe may have taken place on a nearby island some miles away around the same time period.

Playful Young Girl

There have also been sightings of a young girl running around the house, calling out to caretakers and visitors or waving at them. She is likely the daughter of one of the keepers who died at the lighthouse. Records indicate that a young girl was buried on the island. Her laughter and the sound of her bouncing a ball have also been heard upstairs in the keeper's house. Additionally, the footsteps of a child are frequently heard running upstairs.

The little girl could also be the prankster who tricks some of the lighthouse caretakers. Recently, one caretaker was alone in the keeper's quarters and was coming up from the basement when she found herself locked in from the other side. The lock is a hook and eye latch type, so the hook had been moved and placed inside the hole of the eye latch. No one has an explanation for how that could have happened.

Two female caretakers were working in the keeper's house when one distinctly heard a young female voice call out, "Hello?" outside the building. Thinking some unknown guests were arriving, they put on their boots and went outside, only to find no one around. The little girl seems to enjoy the company of caretakers and visitors.

Seguin Island Light with its most powerful lens for foggy days.

122

Lady Ghost of the Dusk

Hendricks Head Light, Southport, Maine

Hendricks Head Light was built on Southport Island in 1829 to guide vessels to the shipbuilding hub at Wiscasset Harbor. The beacon is located ten miles south of Boothbay Harbor.

The lighthouse is famous for the "miracle baby" rescue. During a winter gale in 1875, Keeper Jarul Marr spotted a schooner on the nearby rocks. The seas were too rough for a rescue, so he lit bonfires to signal for any survivors. He discovered a large bundle of two feather beds tied together, floating toward the shore. When he ripped them apart, he found a box with a crying baby girl inside. All others on the ship had perished in the storm. The baby was aptly named Seaborn, and later adopted by a couple from the area.

Hendricks Head Lighthouse at sunset.

The location is also known for a female ghost who is seen only at dusk. On a cold December afternoon in 1931, a woman dressed in black, carrying the manner and language of someone from high society, stopped at Charlie Pinkham's post office store in Southport and asked his wife for directions to an open stretch of ocean. Mrs. Pinkham replied, "You're near Hendricks Head Lighthouse, but it might be dark by the time you get back, and it's quite lonely." The woman seemed familiar with the area and expressed her gratitude.

It was late in the afternoon as the cold winds continued to blow and the sun began to hide behind thickening clouds, Mrs. Pinkham discussed the incident with her husband. They both felt it seemed a little strange for someone to head to the shoreline with sunset approaching on such a cold day in December. Mrs. Pinkham kept her eye on the road to watch for the woman's return.

It was near dusk when Keeper Charles Knight of Hendricks Head Light arrived at the post office store. Mrs. Pinkham asked him if he had met the woman on the road, but he insisted he hadn't seen anyone. As he listened to the story, he became increasingly worried. Since the road to Hendricks Head was the only route, if she was heading that way, he surely would have seen her. They wondered why such a well-dressed woman would be walking alone along the shoreline in near darkness. Other townsfolk arrived at the store afterwards, and Mrs. Pinkham kept repeating the woman's description. Nobody seemed to know her in this small community of Southport, nor had anyone seen her.

Worried for the woman's safety as twilight approached, Keeper Knight headed back to Hendricks Head Light while keeping a close eye out for her. He knew everyone in the area and felt he could easily spot a stranger if he happened to see someone. Later, he reported noticing something flicker like a shadowy figure near one of the nearby cottages, where he paused, listened, and called out with no response. Assuming it was nothing, he continued on his way to the lighthouse. When he arrived, he told his wife about the young woman. She replied that she hadn't seen anyone on the road.

By the next day, many residents of Southport had heard about the "woman in black" and decided to search for her. In the sandy soil, a short distance from the lighthouse, they discovered footprints believed to belong to a woman. The location of these footprints suggests that Keeper Knight may have walked near her while heading to the post office. It appeared she did not want to be recognized or found and perhaps ran into the woods upon hearing the keeper approach. Many feared she might have waded into the icy water.

Throughout the week, there was no news regarding her whereabouts. They attempted to retrace her steps, but their efforts proved futile. They learned that a woman had checked into the Fullerton Hotel in the harbor under the name Louise Meade, without ever returning. The entire community was now on the lookout for her.

Suspecting something was awry, Charlie Pinkham, a volunteer firefighter in town, gathered a search party that found her body on Sunday, December 6, 1931. It had washed ashore on the ledge at the north end of the small beach near Hendricks Head Lighthouse. She was discovered with a leather belt secured around her wrists and the handles of her handbag. The belt was also threaded through the handles of a large, heavy electric flat iron, which authorities believed was intended to weigh her down in the water. One hand was hooked on the belt while the other rested inside the clasp of her partially opened bag.

Beach by Hendricks Head Light at dusk.

The labels on her clothes, the only identifying marks ever found, were from Lord & Taylor, a trendy store in New York City. However, those labels never provided any assistance. Nobody could uncover any details about her, despite detectives searching tirelessly, and her description and story appeared in newspapers across the nation. The prevailing theory is that she took her own life, and she remains registered in the local medical records as a suicide.

It was also learned that she had asked several people where she could find a good view of the open ocean. In an effort to identify her, those she spoke with came forward during the investigation to share what they knew. Most of the townspeople suggested she visit the wharves of Boothbay Harbor, which seemed to hold no interest for her. As Mrs. Pinkham noted during the investigation, she believed the woman was familiar with Hendricks Head Light and the surrounding area.

The bag left at the Fullerton Hotel, where she registered as Louise Meade, and the one attached to her belt provided no evidence of her identity or origin. Any identification at the hotel may have been carefully removed. No one came forward to provide any information about her.

Finally, on January 8, 1932, after weeks of investigation with no one to identify her or make any claims to the body, the town of Southport buried her in the old cemetery along the road to Hendricks Head. The names on the monuments in this small cemetery included local sea captains, early settlers, and other Southport residents. The town decided to bury this mysterious woman, known as Louise Meade, in their cemetery, slightly off to one side, and provided her with a respectful burial. Today, the only markers are a few field stones placed mainly to indicate the grave site.

Hendricks Head Light on one of its many foggy days.

Over the years, many have reported sightings of her ghost or shadowy figure, primarily at twilight near Hendricks Head Light, earning her the title "Lady Ghost of the Dusk." Sometimes she appears in the moonlight, and some swear they have seen her walking along the beach area by the rocks where she was discovered when the fog rolls in.

There have also been sightings over the years of a black "limousine" driving down Hendricks Head Road and parking near the spot where her body washed ashore. Some say it always appears during the first week of December, marking the anniversary of the death of a woman known only as Louise Meade.

Many stories have emerged about who this woman might be. Her death occurred during the Prohibition Era, a time when smuggling was widely believed to have taken place along the Maine coastline. This led some to speculate that she might have been involved in liquor smuggling, possibly going to the coast that late afternoon in 1931 to signal a liquor boat, or that she may have been murdered because she either knew too much or had betrayed someone. No one knows, and the story remains one of Maine's mysteries.

Same Time Spirits at Burnt Island

Burnt Island Light, Boothbay, Maine

Guarding the entrance to Boothbay Harbor, Burnt Island Light was among the earliest lighthouses constructed in the region to support the growing commerce at the fishing port of Boothbay Harbor. Most keepers enjoyed living on the island because of its close proximity to the mainland. The region was also becoming a bustling hub for shipbuilding and the transportation of materials not only along the coast but also along the mighty Kennebec River near the shipbuilding city of Bath. This area of Maine was part of Massachusetts until it was granted statehood in 1820, and the lighthouse was built in 1821, making it the first lighthouse in the newly (expanded) recognized state of Maine. In 1962, it became the last lighthouse in New England to be converted from kerosene to electricity, and it became one of the last Maine lights to be automated in 1988.

Burnt Island Lighthouse is believed to be haunted by the spirit of a former keeper who continues to help maintain the lighthouse, as well as by the wife of another keeper who died at the station and roams the grounds. Both spirits are said to appear in the early morning around 2 a.m., coinciding with the time of their deaths.

Rocky shore of Burnt Island Lighthouse.

Keeper's Wife in White

Keeper James McCobb was a former sea captain who served at Burnt Island Light from 1868 to 1880. He maintained a detailed logbook, recording storms and ships. He also wrote extensively about special moments with his wife, Martha, whom he loved dearly, and enjoyed his time at the lighthouse.

Years later, after battling lung congestion and the spread of internal cancer, on March 22, 1877, at 2 a.m., Martha passed away at the age of 53. She was buried in the central burial ground in Boothbay the following Sunday. McCobb fell into a deep depression and left the lighthouse service in 1880. Since Martha's death, visitors to the island have reported seeing a woman in a white nightgown, often during the early morning hours, around 2 a.m.

In the late 1950s, Keeper James McCollough's wife, Betty, reported seeing a spirit one evening while waiting for her husband to return with supplies. She noticed a woman dressed in white on the front porch near a lilac bush, and then the figure vanished.

Hank Sieg was the last keeper to serve on Burnt Island. He and his wife, Jeanne, moved to the island in the 1980s with their two children. One night, around 2 a.m., he woke up in bed and saw a woman in a white nightgown walking down the hallway and entering another bedroom. Assuming it was his wife, he closed his eyes and rolled over to enjoy the extra space on the bed, only to discover that his wife was still there, asleep beside him. He went to the other bedroom to investigate and found it empty and icy cold.

Dedicated Keeper with a Bum Leg

Keeper Benjamin Stockbridge cherished life on the island and was dedicated to his daily responsibilities. He held the position from 1950 to 1955. As an older keeper with a bum leg, he began to face health issues that affected his physical duties. The Coast Guard sent a younger man named Reg to the island to assist him with the more demanding tasks. Although the young man was inexperienced in lighthouse tending, Stockbridge was determined to teach him the proper methods for maintaining the light. Eventually, the keeper's health worsened, necessitating round-the-clock hospital care. The young assistant took the keeper and his wife to shore to spend his final days before returning to the lighthouse to carry out the daily tasks he had learned from his mentor.

He performed his duties at the lighthouse as he had been instructed. Days later, the new interim lighthouse keeper was awakened around 2 a.m. by the sound of the front door bursting open and a voice shouting, "The light is out, the light is out! You have a smoke-out!" Reg glanced out the window at the light tower and saw nothing but darkness; the light was indeed out. Dressed only in his nightclothes, he leaped from bed, ran through the covered walkway, and scrambled up the circular staircase to the light beacon. With some effort and ingenuity, he managed to rekindle the lamp and restore the light.

Exhausted from the ordeal, he couldn't comprehend how anyone could have reached the island and raised the alarm. Remembering the initial moments of the incident, he realized that the visitor's voice sounded very much like that of Keeper Benjamin Stockbridge. The next day, Reg went into Boothbay Harbor to meet a local fisherman. When he asked how Ben was doing in the hospital, the fisherman told him that the keeper had died at 2 o'clock that morning.

The next couple of weeks passed as Reg, still working as the interim keeper, was awakened around 2 a.m. He heard footsteps coming from the tower's walkway toward the house. It sounded like someone wearing boots and having a bad leg, like his predecessor. He went into the kitchen, tied a string to the door latch, and held the other end to his wrist while balancing a rifle in his other hand. Uncertain if there was an intruder outside, he waited until the footsteps stopped, then yanked on the string to open the door, but there was no one there.

Reg lay awake all night, fearful of the approaching ghost or any odd sounds, reluctant to believe it was Stockbridge's spirit. The next morning, he carried out his duties at the light, called the Coast Guard station, and stated he would not spend another night on Burnt Island.

In the early 1970s, lighthouse keeper Paul Kelly and his wife were awakened several times in the early morning (around 2 a.m.) by creaking noises, resembling someone walking across the floor. On one occasion, Kelly was disturbed by a loud voice bellowing his last name, which alerted him to an issue with the light. Many caretakers believe that Benjamin Stockbridge still maintains his lighthouse. To this day, some people who work and sleep overnight on the island report their watches stopping precisely at 2:00 a.m. The sounds of footsteps and doors slamming are still being heard.

Woman in White on Ram Island

Ram Island Light, Boothbay, Maine

In 1837, Congress appropriated funds for constructing a lighthouse on Ram Island. However, Captain Joseph Smith of the U.S. Navy declared that building a beacon on Ram Island was unnecessary, as the area had enough lighthouses. Despite the objections of many local mariners who considered the area essential for a functioning light, funding was halted for decades until 1883.

During this period, as more shipwrecks occurred near the island, local fishermen decided to take matters into their own hands. One fisherman began hanging a lantern daily, which helped guide some boats away from the rocky shore until he left the area. Then, a young lobsterman named Aldis McKay chose to continue the tradition, hanging a lantern at night inside a glass box weighed down with rocks to prevent the light from blowing over during storms. A third fisherman maintained the ritual by using a dory, anchoring the small boat and placing the lantern in the bow. Eventually, the dory was destroyed in a storm, and a solitary resident on the island took it upon himself to care for the lantern for a few more years.

Stormy weather at Ram Island Lighthouse.

Stormy, foggy day at Ram Island Light.

However, more accidents and storms followed, and no light was available for some time. During this period, a series of sightings of a "woman in white" emerged, along with other strange events believed to warn mariners against crashing on the shore, thus becoming part of the area's folklore.

Many mariners have reported seeing an apparition of the "woman in white" standing on the rocks, a glowing figure waving her arms to warn ships of the dangers posed by the treacherous rocky shore in the area. She has also been seen waving a bright light, or as brightly illuminated.

One captain recounted hearing a foghorn guiding him during a blizzard, despite the absence of such a device on the island. Another observer witnessed a burning boat, prompting him to quickly change direction; however, there was no evidence of any burning vessel in the area the following day. Unexplained fires were reportedly visible from the rocks, and a schooner helmsman saw a lightning bolt flash as he approached the island on a quiet, foggy night.

Ram Island Light was finally built in 1883 on this rocky island outside of Boothbay Harbor, to guide vessels around Fisherman's Island Passage. After its completion, there were fewer instances of the "woman in white" reported, although, at times, fishermen have claimed she still appears on some foggy or stormy nights.

Shivering Woman in Red And...

Pemaquid Point Light, Bristol, Maine

Pemaquid Point Lighthouse was built to support the growing fishing and lumber industries along the mid-coast of Maine. Constructed in 1827, the lighthouse quickly exhibited signs of significant weathering in its masonry. Upon inspection, it was determined that the mason had utilized seawater in the mortar, leading to the rapid deterioration of the structure.

In 1835, the beacon was disassembled and rebuilt with strict instructions in the new contract to use only fresh water for the masonry to ensure the tower's endurance against the many storms that frequented the coast. A keeper's house was added in 1837.

Pemaquid Point Light became one of the most sought-after locations for many keepers and their families, as it was easily accessible by land and allowed them to raise animals and crops. However, access from the water side was challenging due to the dangerous rock formations along the shore. Lighthouse tenders had to anchor offshore while attempting to transfer supplies from ships. Suppliers needed to crawl over the treacherous rocks in front of the lighthouse and grounds, and sometimes accidents would occur.

Unique and treacherous rock formations by Pemaquid Point Lighthouse.

Pemaquid Point Lighthouse stands atop some of the most scenic yet perilous rock formations, which have caused numerous shipwrecks for mariners. The Fisherman's Museum, located next to the lighthouse tower, was once part of the keeper's quarters. Over the years, reports have surfaced of sightings of a woman's ghost in a red shawl, seen near the fireplace of the keeper's house, staring into the flames. The apparition appears wet and shivering, dressed in period clothing and appearing distressed. Although there is no historical record of anyone dying inside the lighthouse or keeper's building, given the many wrecks that have occurred near the station, she may be one of those who perished in one of those tragedies, or perhaps she is still waiting for a lost love.

Many visitors who rent the keeper's apartment upstairs report experiencing unexplained noises, door slams, faint cries, footsteps, and icy cold spots. There have also been accounts of lights suddenly turning on, even when the tower or house is unoccupied. One visitor mentioned being in the parking lot late at night when every light in the vacant keeper's building abruptly illuminated.

The "ghost hunters" of Maine Ghost Walk who look for strange spikes in electromagnetic field (EMF) activity were contacted to look around the keeper's house. When they had arrived they experienced wild fluctuations on the K2 meter, a type of EMF detector. They also brought in night vision cameras, and video recorders, where they observed and documented paranormal activity. Many believe there is more than one spirit at the lighthouse.

Two Wrecks During a Fierce Storm and a Strange Coincidence

After a dense fog lifted, a violent storm with severe gale-force winds descended upon the region on Thursday, September 16, 1903. During this storm, the fishing schooner *George F. Edmunds*, loaded with its mackerel catch from Gloucester, Massachusetts, attempted to round the point, but the winds were too strong for the sturdy vessel. Captain Willard G. Poole had observed the storm's ferocity approaching and decided to try to reach the small harbor in South Bristol instead of navigating close to the coast and landing in the larger Portland Harbor many miles away. He was the only person with some knowledge of the Pemaquid area and headed for Lighthouse Point near the beacon.

The *George F. Edmunds* was within a mile of the point as the gale-force winds intensified, filling the sails and forcing the ship to drift toward the rocks. The captain miscalculated the drift of the schooner by about 800 feet while trying to navigate around the point to the safety of the little harbor, resulting in the ship being driven against the dangerous rocks near Pemaquid. The vessel began to break apart almost immediately.

The captain ordered the crew to launch the dories. The crashing surf slammed the boats against the nearby rocks as they were lowered over the side. Some crewmen attempted to swim toward shore, but the strength of the tidal undertow pulled them away, and they perished.

One of the dories launched successfully and managed to avoid the rocks as it made its way to shore with five crew members. However, a massive wave capsized the vessel halfway there, leaving the five occupants in the fierce, frigid surf to fight for their lives. Only two of them reached the shore. Of the fifteen men aboard the *George F. Edmunds*, thirteen, including Captain Willard Poole, perished in the storm.

During the same storm, the small coasting schooner *Sadie and Lillie* was en route to Boston but became trapped in the fierce winds. The vessel sought shelter alongside the larger *George F. Edmunds*. It, too, was wrecked against the rocks near the lighthouse. Weston Curtis, a local resident and volunteer lifesaver, witnessed the disaster near the lighthouse grounds. He managed to get a line to the *Sadie and Lillie* amidst the raging surf. Captain Willard C. Harding stayed on board to try and free the schooner but soon realized it was futile. The captain then attempted to use the line to reach the shore, but it got tangled in the rocks, leading to his tragic demise in the tumultuous waters.

When the storm subsided the next day, all that remained of the two vessels was splintered wood and twisted iron where they had wrecked. Seven months after the wreck of the *George F. Edmunds*, Captain Poole's body was found washed ashore on April 1, 1904. The site of the shipwreck, where he had perished, was only three miles from his birthplace in Bristol, Maine.

A young man named William P. Sawyer who lived in Boston spent many summers with his family vacationing at Pemaquid Point. Hearing about the tragedies of the two ships on September 16, he located the two survivors of the *George F. Edmunds* and interviewed them, where he published their stories for the public. He was also a student at Harvard Law School, in the same years as Franklin D. Roosevelt, and became a Boston lawyer. However, he preferred visiting Pemaquid over the years and loved its rural community. When his parents died, he gave up his practice in 1930, and moved to Pemaquid.

After the lighthouse was automated, he found work as the caretaker of the lighthouse and its grounds for fifteen years, during which he was allowed to stay in a nearby cottage. He conducted historical tours for visitors, collected fees in the parking lot, and maintained the grounds for the town of Bristol.

Igneous and metamorphic layered rocks leading to Pemaquid Point Light.

As a strange coincidence, 42 years later, on the anniversary of the shipwrecks on September 16, 1945, Sawyer's body was found washed up on the rocks near Pemaquid Lighthouse. It appeared that the now 66-year-old had committed suicide with a borrowed shotgun from a neighbor. Family members believed it might have been murder, as he had never shown any reason for committing such a self-inflicted act. Townsfolk were divided over why he would take his own life or why anyone would want to murder him, given there was no robbery at his house or signs of struggle, and he was not in a depressed state of mind. The autopsy concluded that investigators believed Sawyer went down to the rocky edge, put the gun in his mouth, and used his toe to pull the trigger. No note as to the reasoning for his act was ever found, nor was the gun.

Running Teenager and Attacker

Marshall Point Light, Port Clyde, Maine

I n the 1800s, Port Clyde became a bustling shipping port for granite, timber, and fishing, as well as a haven for writers and artists, which it still is today. Marshall Point Lighthouse was constructed in 1832 to accommodate traffic entering and leaving Port Clyde Harbor. This location is where Tom Hanks ended up after running cross country in the movie Forrest Gump in 1994.

The keeper who served the station for the longest period was Charles Clement Skinner. He was a Civil War veteran who tended Marshall Point Light from 1874 to 1919. This became the longest tenure of any keeper at the same beacon in the Lighthouse Service history!

The keeper's building which is now a museum of artifacts is rumored to be haunted by a friendly spirit. Former caretakers and museum visitors report hearing footsteps and doors closing in empty rooms. Some who have stayed overnight at the lighthouse claim that a female ghostly apparition sometimes appears and tucks them in at night. On a darker side, there have been sightings on the road leading to the lighthouse of a teenage boy's spirit being chased.

Marshall Point Light with keeper's quarters, which is believed to be haunted.

Teenager Running From Attacker

Ben Bennett was the younger of two boys born to parents of Scandinavian heritage. His father, a fisherman, favored Ben over his brother, had a quick temper, and was abusive toward his mother. Ben lost his mother when he turned twelve; she finally decided she had enough of her husband's abuse, jumped off the wharf on a wintry night, and drowned. Struggling to cope with his grief, Ben got into fights and skipped school. He began to hang out with a tough group of teenagers who frequently clashed with local authorities.

During the Prohibition era of the 1920s, when alcohol was illegal nationwide, smugglers and rum runners flourished, transporting illicit cargo along the coast to various regions of the country. During this time, Ben was walking with his friends down the road toward the lighthouse on a moonlit evening. They noticed a light in the woods and decided to check it out. Taking a path that led to a marsh in the outer harbor, the boys stumbled upon a small group of armed men unloading kegs of booze in a secluded area. Realizing the men were dangerous smugglers, they turned and fled back into the woods.

One of the men with a dark beard, dressed in black and wearing boots, noticed the boys in that exact moment and began to chase them, brandishing a knife. The boys scattered in different directions, but the attacker focused on Ben. When the young lad re-emerged onto Marshall Point Road, the smuggler caught up with him and stabbed him in the back, killing him. He returned from his gruesome act to his fellow smugglers, who quickly replaced the cargo into the boat and left the area before anyone could identify them.

Some years later, a family with two daughters were walking down the road to the lighthouse. Suddenly, they heard footsteps pounding behind them some distance away. When they turned to look back, they saw a young man being chased by a larger, older man dressed in black. The frightened family began running for their lives, with the father picking up the youngest girl so she wouldn't fall behind. They rounded a corner, and the sound of footsteps faded away. When one of the girls glanced back, she noticed that no one was there.

Over the years, reports have emerged about sightings of the ghost of Ben Bennett. He is often seen running along the road, sometimes pursued by a large, bearded man in dressed in black, holding a knife. Both figures seem to vanish as they turn the corner.

Old Captain and the Little Lady

Owls Head Light, Owls Head, Maine

The booming lime trade in Rockland and nearby Thomaston necessitated the establishment of Owls Head Light at the entrance to Rockland Harbor. In addition to fishing, other industries included granite quarrying, steamship transportation, and even ice harvesting, which made Rockland Harbor one of the busiest locations on the Maine coast. Built in 1826 and authorized by President John Quincy Adams, the lighthouse has witnessed numerous shipwrecks. Though only 20 feet tall, its tower is perched on a high cliff, positioning the lantern beam over 100 feet above the water.

War of 1812 veteran Isaac Stearns was appointed as its first keeper. His wife, Lucy, had a narrow escape one day while heading to the tower to trim the wicks. When she reached the tower, a powerful gust of wind nearly sent her over the cliff and into the sea.

Recently, Coastal Living magazine recognized Owls Head Light as the most haunted lighthouse in America. Two spirits are said to inhabit the lighthouse. One is believed to be the friendly spirit of a former lighthouse keeper known for his diligent nature. The second entity is known as the "Little Lady. "

Owls Head Lighthouse over rocky cliffs.

Old Sea Captain Keeper

Some keepers were so dedicated to protecting mariners that many locals believed their spirits remained at the light station they cherished, never abandoning their post even in death. Many of these keepers had once been ship captains. At Owls Head Light, numerous reports have documented mysterious footprints resembling those left by a large pair of work boots that appeared after rain or snowfall. The tracks typically led in only one direction: up the ramp, stairs, and to the tower, where the brass was polished and the lens cleaned. Over the years, some keepers visited the tower only to find the door open, and the brass and lens had been mysteriously polished.

In the mid-1980s, Andy Germann served as a Coast Guard keeper at Owls Head Light with his wife, Denise. At that time, the lighthouse was undergoing renovations, and one night, after going to bed, he decided to step outside to ensure that some construction materials were securely stored. As he left the bedroom, he noticed a faint cloud of smoke hovering in front of him before passing through his body. Although he found this rather strange, he continued to check on the materials.

Moments later, his wife, Denise, felt someone getting back into bed, assuming it was her husband. She asked, "How'd you make out outside?" When she received no reply, she turned to see a shifting indentation in the bed beside her, but nobody was there. She then spoke sharply for it to go away so she could sleep, and the movement ceased as she drifted off again. The following day, the keeper told his wife about the hovering cloud while she recounted her encounter that had happened around the same time.

Gerard Graham managed the station in the late 1980s with his wife Debbie and their young daughter Claire. The Grahams were told about the resident ghost by the Germanns. The previous keepers mentioned that the smallest room upstairs was the most "active," but due to limited space, the Grahams chose to put Claire in that little room, not believing the stories. They stayed in the larger bedroom nearby.

While the Grahams lived at the station for a couple of years, little Claire beleived she had an imaginary friend she called the "old sea captain." She described him as a man with a beard, dressed in a blue coat and a seaman's cap, even though her parents were sure that no such person existed.

One night, Claire burst into her parents' room and yelled, "The fog's rolling in! Time to turn on the foghorn!" Gerard and Debbie were taken aback, as they had never heard her use such language before. They went outside and saw that the fog was indeed rolling in. They decided to heed their daughter's warning and activated the foghorn to alert local mariners. Whatever this entity was, the Grahams felt no fear, and their daughter seemed to enjoy the company of the "old captain." This presence also appeared to be quite fond of and friendly toward the little girl.

Waterside view of Owls Head Lighthouse station over rocky cliffs.

The Little Lady

The other spirit at the lighthouse is the "Little Lady." Her ghostly figure is often seen in the kitchen or out the window. Doors slam throughout the house, and silverware rattles in the drawers; however, anyone encountering her feels a sense of peace. She is likely the wife of one of the former keepers who resided there, as her love for the station was so strong that she never wanted to leave, even in death.

In the late 1980s, Malcolm Rouse was the last Coast Guard keeper. One night his wife, noticed the silhouette of a woman in white through the kitchen window. On several occasions, their son would also tell his parents he saw a short woman wearing white clothing sitting in a chair in his room. No one however, felt threatened by her presence.

Grumpy Ghost of the Tower

Matinicus Rock Light, Matinicus, Maine

Matinicus Rock Light is located on a small rocky island about five miles from Matinicus Island in Penobscot Bay. The lighthouse is situated approximately 18 miles from the nearest mainland and about 25 miles from the port of Rockland, Maine. Initially built in 1827 as two lighthouses to accommodate the increasingly busy shipping traffic around Penobscot Bay, many of its keepers fell ill, with some dying, due to what many believe was the constant cold, damp air and frequent storms sweeping over the island.

The lighthouse is famous for its teenage heroine, Abby Burgess, who in 1853, helped save her family from destructive storms for nearly four weeks while her father, Keeper Samuel Burgess, was trapped on the mainland. During her family's stay, the station originally had two towers: a north tower and a south tower. Today, only the south tower has remained active while the north tower was decommissioned in 1924 and locked up, which has helped to keep a grumpy spirit inside.

Matinicus Rock Lighthouse: North tower is capped in front, active south tower connected to keeper's building behind.

Although no documented record of any suicide at the station exists, there is a story about an unknown assistant lighthouse keeper at Matinicus Rock, unable to bear the desolation and isolation of such a remote and barren place, climbed to the north tower, tied a rope around his neck, and hanged himself. His death was discovered a few days later when the residents of Matinicus Island, a few miles away, noticed that the light hadn't been turned on.

Regardless, there have been reports from keepers and Coast Guardsmen about an agitated spirit or shadowy figure lurking around the north tower and the keeper's house. Some believe the entity could have been a former keeper that had died from sickness at the station. They observed broken dishes, overturned chairs, and supplies in disarray. Those stationed there eventually discovered how to stop the haunting by locking and barring the door to the tower.

After that, there were no reported sightings, strange noises, or paranormal activities until, one day, a crewman needed to retrieve materials from the tower. When he opened the door, mechanical problems began to affect the station. The light malfunctioned, machinery broke down, and the foghorn emitted an unusual sound. The tower is now always kept locked. As long as the door remains secured, the lighthouse stays quiet.

In the early 1950s, a Coast Guard officer arrived at Matinicus Rock for an inspection. After hearing the ghost story from those stationed at the lighthouse, he insisted that the crew abandon their superstitious nonsense and unlock the door. They followed his orders, and that night, all the lights on the island went out. The crew locked the door to the north tower once again, and the lighthouse has not faced any issues.

Kevin J. Arsenault, a Coast Guardsman stationed at the lighthouse from 1976 to 1977, reported a resident ghost locked in the north tower, named "Moe" by earlier personnel. Arsenault noted that he often observed a glow emanating from the abandoned tower, despite the absence of electricity or lights within.

Capped north tower of Matinicus Rock Light.

142

Foreign Woman of the House

Narragaugus (Pond Island) Light, Milbridge, Maine

Narraguagus (Pond island) Lighthouse was built in 1853 to accommodate the shipping traffic, primarily of lumber from the Narraguagus River into the harbor at Milbridge. The keeper's building has been the site of some paranormal activity involving a protective foreign female ghost, who disapproves of any changes made to the house.

Narragaugus (Pond Island) Light on rocky shoreline.

In the 1970s, two college friends of the Dameron family, who were staying at the lighthouse, spent the night in a downstairs bedroom to help with renovations that week. They were suddenly awakened by a woman's angry voice speaking in a foreign language. The only woman in the house was Nancy Dameron, the owner, who spoke only English. The following night, one of the young men heard a loud noise beside him, as if something heavy had fallen near his pillow, but he saw nothing. Both boys got up and insisted that they were there only to help fix the house, not to harm it. For the rest of their stay, the room remained quiet.

Vengeful Worker and Other Spirits

Bass Harbor Head Light, Tremont, Maine

Bass Harbor Head Lighthouse was established in 1858 to assist mariners in navigating the treacherous Bass Harbor Bar and guiding them into Blue Hill Bay. The station initially featured a hand-rung fog bell, later replaced in 1898 by a 4,000-pound fog bell equipped with specialized striking machinery that still stands beside the lighthouse, alongside the original oil house. The lighthouse rises 56 feet above the water on rocky cliffs in Acadia National Park and is one of America's most photographed and iconic beacons. It is said that the lighthouse is haunted by a vengeful construction worker, among other spirits.

Bass Harbor Head Lighthouse over rocky cliffs.

When construction began on the lighthouse in 1858, one worker suddenly vanished from his duties and was never heard from again. Sometimes, workers either do not get along with their coworkers, or the work itself is too difficult, or they have other issues that may cause them to walk off the site. Very little is known about this person, but it is reported that his coworkers found a bloodied axe hidden near the construction site, with no explanation as to how the blood

144

appeared. As some stories go, it seems a page may have been taken from an Edgar Allan Poe tale (The Cask of Amontillado). Many believe the missing worker is entombed within the foundation walls of either the tower or the keeper's house. It's possible that he was killed after an argument with a coworker, after which his body was concealed inside the walls and then cemented over.

Though the worker was never found, and no one was held accountable for the possible crime, it appears the spirit has taken its vengeance on keepers and caretakers over the years by attacking their bodies. Many have succumbed to lethal diseases like typhoid fever, or have experienced long term sicknesses, heart attacks, or strokes. Still others have been involved in strange accidents like falling off ladders, having severe cuts, or have fallen onto the rocks below.

The lighthouse's location offers an extraordinary view of the ocean below the rocky cliffs, making this one of the more desirable places for a lighthouse keeper and his family to live. However, what adds fuel to the story is that most keepers only stayed at the station for a few years, and many fell very ill while stationed there, which is quite strange. It has been reported that there have been ten tragic deaths near the beacon.

There are reports of other paranormal activity in and by the lighthouse. Some have claimed to have seen an apparition of a man sitting on a stump or log outside when it is snowing. A female entity has been witnessed rocking in a chair through one of the windows of the keeper's house. Other people have seen a large deer prancing through the snow towards the lighthouse, and then the animal disappears. When observers go out to look for tracks, none can be found.

Multiple spirits at Bass Harbor light.

Captain Salty and Turning Statue

Prospect Harbor Light, Prospect Harbor, Maine

The region has always been one of the foggiest on the northern Maine coast. Prospect Harbor has been a busy fishing harbor since the mid-1800s. Prospect Harbor Lighthouse was initially built in 1850 of granite, then rebuilt in 1891 of wood, to guide local traffic of coasting schooners and fishermen. The local fishing industry always determined the existence of the beacon. Today, the active lighthouse guides mostly lobster and sardine fishermen to and from their homes.

Currently, the station functions as a satellite military installation. The keeper's quarters, known as Gull Cottage, is reserved exclusively for military personnel. Over the years, guests and caretakers have reported an apparition belonging to possibly a previous keeper, the strong scent of pipe tobacco, and have observed an out of reach statue constantly turning different directions.

Prospect Harbor Lighthouse on a typical foggy day in Maine.

Father's Pipe Tobacco

Albion Faulkingham was the last keeper of the light, serving from 1930 until 1934, when the light was automated. Shortly thereafter, John Workman became the property's caretaker and lived in the dwelling until 1953. On New Year's Day in 1951, Workman's father, Ira Workman, tragically passed away at the lighthouse from a heart attack he suffered while lighting his pipe.

Over the years, many who have stayed in the keeper's quarters have reported experiencing the strong scent of pipe tobacco from what is believed to be the spirit of Ira Workman when no one else is smoking in the building.

Captain Salty

A former lighthouse keeper's ghost is also believed to haunt Gull Cottage, who some call Captain Salty. Some visitors have heard footsteps on the stairs and claimed to have seen a ghostly figure at night flowing between the walls. Reports have also circulated of doors opening and closing, lights flickering on and off, and various other strange occurrences.

One story involves a couple putting their son to bed. The father says goodnight, and then the very excited boy asks, "Who are you?" The confused parent replies, "I'm Daddy." The boy responds, "No, who's that behind you?" The couple look at one another, then look in the direction the boy is pointing behind his parents, but there is no one there. There have been no investigations to determine who the keeper is, although some believe it may be Ira Workman, the same person who is the source of the pipe tobacco smell.

Statue of the Little Captain Turning

The most frequent activity observed involves a little statue. On a windowsill, lined up above the stairs out of reach of guests, are three small figurine statues of nautical or maritime men wearing coats, caps, and trousers standing on blocks of wood. They are usually turned to face the ocean. One of the small statues is of a sea captain wearing a dark wool coat and a tie. He is placed in the center, but appears to be consistently turning to face the stairs one moment (maybe when curious on the happenings in the house) and, at another time, guests notice that the statue is turned to face the sea.

Driving Directions to
Haunted Lighthouses and Boat Docks

Some of these beacons are on the mainland. However, many of these lighthouses are offshore, and directions are also provided to the docks on the mainland to take boats out to these lighthouses. Boat cruises have different tours, and some are specific lighthouse cruises for those wanting to view many beacons in a given trip. More information can be found on my website at NELights.com.

Connecticut

Sheffield Island Light, Norwalk, Connecticut
Driving directions to the Ferry.
The ferry boat from the Norwalk Seaport Association provides daily service to Sheffield Island where the lighthouse is a few hundred feet from the dock. From the West: Take US I-95 North and Exit 14 to South Norwalk for about a quarter mile. Turn right onto Fairfield Avenue for about half a mile, where Fairfield Avenue becomes West Washington Street, and continue for another half mile. Turn right onto Water Street or Route 136 to the dock.

Penfield Reef Light, Fairfield, Connecticut
Driving directions for a distant view: Lighthouse can be seen from Seaside Park en route to Black Rock Harbor Lighthouse.
Take Exit 27 off Route 95 to Lafayette Boulevard to South Ave., left at Park Ave, and park at Seaside Park.
There are currently no public boat tours available out to the lighthouse.

Stratford Shoal (Middleground) Light, Bridgeport, Connecticut
Unable to view from the shore, and no public boat tours are available.

New London Ledge Light, New London, Connecticut
Driving directions for a distant view.
From US Route I-95 North, take Exit 86 (US Route 1) to Defense Highway (Route 349). From US Route I-95 South, take Exit 87 to Route 349, then Left on Rainville Ave., left on Eastern Point Road. Follow into Shennecossett Road, then turn right onto Beach Pond Road. Bear left onto Rita Santa Croce Drive to Eastern Point Park. The lighthouse can also be viewed from Shore Ave.
Driving directions to boat dock: New London Maritime Society provides boat tours out to the lighthouse.
From US Route I-95 North, Take Exit 83 onto CT 32 toward North Norwich/New London Waterfront District. Turn right onto Jay Street, left onto Blinman Street, right onto Bank Sreet. Dock is on the left.

Rhode Island

Block Island Southeast Light, Block Island, Rhode Island
Driving directions to dock: Block Island Ferry from Point Judith to Block Island.
From Route I-95 North: Take Exit 92 in Connecticut. Bear right onto North
Stonington Road, CT-Route 2. Look for right-hand turn for RI-Route 78 East toward
Westerly. At the end of RI-Route 78, go left onto RI-Route 1 North. Travel on Route
1 North (approx. 19 miles) until the Narragansett/Point Judith exit, Route 108. Take
a right off the exit ramp onto Woodruff Ave. At the second traffic light, bear right
onto Route 108 South (Point Judith Road) for approx. 3.8 miles, there will be a Block
Island Ferry sign. Turn right onto Galilee Escape Road, and at the end turn left onto
Great Island Road. The Block Island Ferry will be on the right-hand side.

From the ferry dock on Block Island: Take Water Street to the rotary and then Spring
Street to Southeast Light Road to the light.

Watch Hill Light, Westerly, Rhode Island
Driving directions: From Route 1A in Avondale, stay on Watch Hill Road, right at
Wauwinnett Street, left at Bay Street, park your car, then walk left on Larkin Street to
Lighthouse Road.

Conimicut Shoal Light, Warwick, Rhode Island
*Driving directions for close view: Conimicut Lighthouse can be seen best from
Conimicut Point Park in Warwick.*
Follow Route 117 East on along the Providence River to Shawomet. Turn eastward
onto Economy Avenue and then make a sharp left onto Symonds Avenue. Turn right
onto Point Avenue and follow it to its end at the park.

Rose Island Light, Newport, Rhode Island
Driving directions for Jamestown Newport Ferry to reach lighthouse in Newport Harbor:
From Route 4 South toward Route 403/Narragansett/Quonset onto US 1 South.
Slight right onto the Route 138 East ramp to Jamestown/Newport. Keep left to
continue on Route 138 East. Take the Helm Street exit and turn right onto Helm
Street, right onto Hull Street, right onto Seaside Drive, right onto Spirketing Street,
then turn right onto Beacon Ave until you reach Ferry Street at the dock.

Save the Bay Tours Organization for lighthouse and coastal preservation provides
an extensive all day Ultimate Lighthouse Tour covering most of the lighthouses in
Narragansett Bay. They leave out of Providence, Rhode Island.
Driving directions to dock: From Route I-95 North or South, take Exit 35 on Thurbers
Avenue to US Route 1A and turn right onto Allens Ave into Cranston, where it
becomes Narragansett Blvd. Turn left onto Harborside Blvd. at the traffic light by
the Shell gas station. Follow Harborside Blvd until the end. Right onto Save The Bay
Drive.

Massachusetts

Borden Flats Light, Fall River, Massachusetts
Driving directions distant view. Take Exit 5 off Route 95 to Route 138 (Broadway) to Bradford, then right at Almond Street to Borden Light Marina.

Cape Cod (Highland) Light, Truro, Massachusetts
Driving directions: Take Route 6 through Truro to Cape Cod Light\Highland exit, take South Highland Road, then left on Lighthouse Road.

Plymouth (Gurnet) Light, Plymouth, Massachusetts
Driving directions: Lighthouse is not open to the general public. However, there may be occasional open houses, and during Duxbury's Opening of the Bay festival in May. Heading south on Route 3A in Marshfield, take Route MA 139 East along Tremont Street and Careswell Street. Take a right onto Canal Street onto Gurnet Road, take right on Mandeville Ave then left onto Plymouth Ave, and left onto Willoughby Lane.

Scituate Light, Scituate, Massachusetts
Driving directions: Take Route 3 North, to Route 53, to Route 123 North (Country Way). Take right at Stockbridge Street, then right at First Parish, left at Front Street, right at Jericho Street, then right at Lighthouse Road.

Minot's Ledge Light, Cohasset, Massachusetts
The lighthouse is too far offshore, and no public boat tours are available

Long Island Head Light and Boston Harbor Light, Boston, Massachusetts
Driving directions to dock for lighthouse cruise by Boston Harbor Islands Organization: Follow I-93 South to John F Fitzgerald Surface Road in Boston. Take Exit 17 from I-93 South. Follow John F Fitzgerald Surface Road to Atlantic Ave.

Driving directions to Boston's Rowes Wharf for Harbor Cruises to the lighthouses: Heading East towards Boston, Take US Route I-90 EAST (Massachusetts Turnpike) to I-93/South station exit towards Concord NH/Quincy. Continue towards South Station, Exit 24A, then continue on to Atlantic Avenue to docks.

Bakers Island Light, Salem, Massachusetts
Driving directions to Salem ferry dock for boat of the Essex National Heritage Area to Bakers Island. Continue on I-95 South to Peabody. Take exit 40A from Route 128 North. Continue on Route 114 East/Andover St. Take right onto Gardner Street, right onto Margin Street onto North Street. Turn right onto Route 107 North/Bridge Street (signs for Beverly), stay on Bridge Street and right on Webb Street, right on Essex Street, and left on Becket Street to 10 Blaney Street in Salem.

New Hampshire

White Island (Isles of Shoals) Light, Rye, New Hampshire

Driving directions to Rye Harbor State Marina: Take Us Route 95 North, then take Exit 2, (at the Hampton Toll Booths). When you come out of the remote toll booth, take the left fork, this is for Route 101 East for about a 1/2 mile. Exit onto Route 27. At end of exit turn right onto Route 27 East. Stay on Route 27 until it ends at the ocean (3.6 miles). You are now at Route 1A. Turn Left and take Rt. 1A North approx. 5.3 miles until you come to Rye Harbor on the right.

Take the Uncle Oscar, from Granite State Whale Watch and Island Cruises to Star Island for a nice view of the lighthouse. They also pass by relatively close to the beacon.

Portsmouth Harbor Light, Portsmouth, New Hampshire

Driving directions: From Interstate 95 in Portsmouth, take Exit 5 and go south on Route 1 Bypass for a little over two miles. Turn left on Elwyn Road, and continue for about a mile and a half until the road ends. Turn left onto Sagamore and then right onto Wentworth Road, which is Route 1B. After about two miles on Route 1B, you will see signs directing you to turn right to the Coast Guard Station of Portsmouth Harbor and Fort Constitution. Park in the Fort Constitution parking lot and walk to the fort during daylight hours from where you can get a good view of the lighthouse. While enjoying this historic fort. The lighthouse tower is closed to the public, but is accessible during open houses offered by Friends of Portsmouth Harbor Lighthouse.

Note: Follow down the road (Route 1B) a short distance to New Castle Commons Park for another view of Portsmouth Harbor Light, and Whaleback Light of Maine across the river. It is one of the rare locations where you see two lighthouses on state borders.

There are also boat cruises that pass by Portland Harbor Light and out to White Island (Isles of Shoals) Light from the Portsmouth docks, many by the Isles of Shoals Steamship Company.

Driving directions: To find the dock, from Route I-95 North take Exit 5 to the Portsmouth Traffic Circle. From I-95 South, take NH Exit 7, then LEFT at lights. At the traffic circle, take your second right on to the Route 1 Bypass North (Towards Maine). Take the 2nd exit onto Maplewood Avenue and make a right at the end of the ramp. Proceed to first set of lights and take a left onto Deer Street. Follow Deer Street to the end, take a left at the stop sign and the Isles of Shoals Steamship Company dock is located on the right just after the salt pile across from the Sheraton Harborside.

For Portsmouth Harbor Cruises, just past the Sheraton Hotel on your right, you will see a small alley on your left marked "Private Way and the "Olde Harbour District". This is Ceres Street where you'll find the dock.

Maine

Cape Neddick (Nubble Light) Lighthouse, York, Maine

Driving directions: Take Exit 4 off I-95 in York to Route 1, then take Route 1A to York Beach (called Long Sands Beach). When you get to the beach's north end, take Nubble Road to the end of Sohier Park Road.

Boon Island Light, York, Maine

Driving directions to boat launch on Kennebunk docks: This remote lighthouse can be accessed through New England Eco Adventures. From I-95 North, Take Exit 19 for Route 9/ME-109 toward Wells/Sanford. Turn left onto ME-109 South/Route 9 East. Turn left onto US-1 North/Post Rd (Pass by M&T Bank on the right). Turn right onto Route 9 East, then turn right onto Harbor Lane.

Cape Porpoise (Goat Island) Light, Kennebunkport, Maine

Driving directions for a distant view: Take the Kennebunkport exit off of I-95, then take Route 35 east until you reach Kennebunk. From US Route 1, take Highway 9E through Kennebunkport. Bear right at the fork by the Cape Porpoise Post Office onto Wharf Street to the fishing pier, where you can view the lighthouse from afar. New England Eco Adventures mentioned above also has a boat tour to the lighthouse.

Wood Island Light, Biddeford, Maine

Driving directions to Vines Landing boat launch: The Friends of Wood Island Lighthouse (FOWL) offers daily water shuttles and tours of Wood Island.
From US I-95 take Exit 32. Go straight through the first light (Route 111) to the second light and turn left onto Route 1. From US Route 1, in Biddeford, take Route 111. Take a right at the lights to Route 9/208 South toward Biddeford Pool for about five miles. Take a left at the end and bear right past the fire station. When you pass Hatties Restaurant, the road bears right. Mile Stretch Road. meets L.B. Orcutt Blvd at the top of the rise. Turn left on L.B. Orcutt, and then go over the rise and straight down the hill a couple of hundred yards; Vine's Landing is right behind the Red Geranium Store, where you can park on the road using the parking signs.
Driving directions for a very distant view of the lighthouse:
Go past the fire station a 1/2-mile till you see a fence on the left before the road bends sharply to the right. The gate entrance is on the left side. Park on the street. Follow a footpath for 1/2 mile alongside the golf course until you come to a rocky shoreline from which you will be able to see the light from a distance.

Cape Elizabeth Light, Cape Elizabeth, Maine

Driving directions: From US I-95 take Exit 45 to US Route 1 North. Take Route 207 South (Black Point Rd.) in Scarborough. Follow to Route 77 North towards Cape Elizabeth (about 5.5 miles). Take a right onto Two Lights Road, past Two Lights State Park, then bear left and continue straight for about a mile till you come to a parking lot by the shore. The lighthouses are to the left of the lot.

Portland Head Light, Cape Elizabeth, Maine

Driving directions: From US Route 1 North outside of Portland to 1A take Route 77 South through South Portland till you come to Shore Road on the left. Follow along until you arrive at Fort Williams State Park on the left.

Seguin Island Light, Georgetown, Maine

Driving directions to boat launch: Fish 'N Trips provides near-daily ferry service to the island. From Bath, take US Route 1 South, then turn right onto Winslow Court, then right onto Court Street, then right onto High Street. Take a slight left onto ME-209 South/Bridge Street. Stay on Routh 209 to Fort Popham State Historic Site, 219 Popham Rd, Phippsburg. Note: Maine Maritime Museum also has tours from Bath.

Burnt Island Light, Boothbay Harbor, Maine

Driving directions to Boothbay dock: Many boat tours leave the dock at Boothbay Harbor and pass by Burnt Island lighthouse. Balmy Days Cruises Provides special access for 3-hour tours to Burnt Island; highly recommended. From Bath, take US Route 1 South, then take the exit toward Congress Ave. At the traffic circle, take the 2nd exit onto State Road, then take the ramp onto US-1 North. Turn right onto Route 27 South, and stay on the route at the traffic circle. Take a slight right onto Oak Street, onto Commercial Street, then left onto Wharf Street. The dock is on the right.

Ram Island Light, Boothbay Harbor, Maine

Driving directions for a distant view: You can reach Boothbay Harbor along Route 27 from Route 1. Take a left on Route 96 from Route 27 in Boothbay and follow it for about 10 miles to the end and you'll be treated to a special area referred to as Ocean Point, where you'll find yourself driving along the edge of the shoreline with Ram Island Lighthouse a short distant view away.
Balmy Days Cruises, and Cap'n Fish's Whale Watch and Scenic Nature Cruises, among others, provide boat cruises past Ram Island Light, Burnt Island Light, and others. Use dock directions for Burnt Island Light.

Hendricks Head Light, Southport, Maine

Driving directions: From US Route 1, after crossing the bridge at Wiscasset, take Route 27 South through Boothbay Harbor towards Southport. You'll find Lakeside Drive on the right about ten miles from Boothbay. After about 2 1/2 miles when you round a curve, you'll see a small rotary around a monument by Southport Grocery Store. Take that sharp right in front of the store and then follow Beech Road for about 3 miles till you come upon the lighthouse. It is privately owned now, but there is a small beach just before it where you can park and get a close view the lighthouse.

Pemaquid Point Light, Bristol, Maine

Driving directions: From the Highway US Route 1 Business Route in Damariscotta turn south on Highway 129 and drive for just under three miles to the intersection of Highways 129 and 130. Take Highway 130 south for about 12 miles to Pemaquid Point, where you will see the lighthouse by a large parking lot.

Marshall Point Light, Port Clyde, Maine

Driving directions: From US Route 1 in Thomaston, take Route 131 South to Port Clyde. At the main intersection, turn left, then take a right immediately after the restaurant. The unmarked but paved Marshall Point Road will lead you a mile to a tiny parking lot at Marshall Point Light.

Owls Head Light, Owls Head, Maine

Driving directions: From US Route 1 in Rockland, take Route 73 to North Shore Drive and turn left there. Keep going until you reach the Owls Head Post Office, turn left there, and follow to Lighthouse Road on the left. This will bring you to the parking lot of Lighthouse Park. A short walk along a dirt road from the parking lot will lead you to Owls Head Light.

Matinicus Rock Light, Matinicus, Maine

To access this very remote lighthouse, Matinicus Excursions provides a water taxi, that can take you from the mainland at Rockland to Matinicus Island, then to Matinicus Rock Light, about five miles away from Matinicus Island. Staying on Matinicus island is amazing and highly recommended if you want to disconnect and feel like 50 years before.

Driving directions to dock: To find the dock at Rockland, follow US Route 1 North into Rockland as Maine Street. Turn right onto Front Street, and the public landing is there.

Bass Harbor Head Light, Tremont, Mount Desert Island, Maine

Driving directions: From US Route 1 in Ellsworth, take Route 3 onto Mount Desert Island (this is Acadia National Park). Bear right onto Route 102 and follow south bearing right onto Route 102A to the parking lot by the lighthouse.

Prospect Harbor Light, Prospect Harbor, Maine

Driving directions: You cannot go onto the lighthouse grounds because of security reasons, as it is part of a military installation. To get to the lighthouse, from US Route 1 take 186 to Prospect Harbor. Turn right on 195 then bear right at the fork onto Lighthouse Point Rd. You can view the light off from the shoreline outside of the gates. Another view is from Winter Harbor on Route 186, enter Prospect Harbor and look for Stinson Canning Company. You can get a view just off the grounds; feel free to visit the company for some canned fish products. Another view is from Lighthouse Point Road leading to the restricted Navy station. Drive past a sign the reads "Detachment Alpha" to where Route 195 bears a left towards Corea.

Narraguagus (Pond Island) Light, Milbridge, Maine

Driving directions to boat dock: Robertson Sea Tours has a special lighthouse cruise covering Narraguagus (Pond Island) Light. Take US Route 1 North onto Bay View Road in Milbridge, the dock will be on the right.

Selected Bibliography

Below is a sampling of newspaper articles, books, and websites, used for this book. Many of the historical accounts were taken from newspapers.

"Keeper of Penfield Reef Lighthouse Drowned." Norwich Bulletin. December 26, 1916, sec. 1.

Barry, Richard. "New London Lighthouse Allegedly Haunted by a Ghost Named Ernie." 1420 WBSM, March 31, 2023. https://wbsm.com/new-london-lighthouse-haunted-ghost-ernie/?utm_source=tsmclip&utm_medium=referral.

Roberts, Bruce, Cheryl Shelton-Roberts, and Ray Jones. *American Lighthouses: A Comprehensive Guide to Exploring Our National Coastal Treasures.* Guilford, CT: Globe Pequot, 2012.

USCG: Frequently Asked Questions." U. S. Coast Guard Home Page. https://www.uscg.mil/history

Scott, Kirsti. "The Ghost Bride of Crescent Beach." Beachcombing Magazine, February 20, 2024. https://www.beachcombingmagazine.com/blogs/news/the-ghost-bride-of-crescent-beach.

"Top 5 Most Haunted Lighthouses in Massachusetts." GhostQuest.net. https://www.ghostquest.net/blog/top-5-most-haunted-lighthouses-in-massachusetts.

D'Entremont, Jeremy. 2020 / US Lighthouse Society. *New England's Haunted Lighthouses.* October 31. https://www.youtube.com/watch?v=FCX-0NFdUJM.

Walks, American Ghost. "Maine's Haunted Lighthouses: Ghost Stories & Legends." A white background with a few lines on it, December 31, 2024. https://www.americanghostwalks.com/articles/maine-haunted-lighthouses.

Writer, Staff. "Goat Island Keeper Haunted Light Following Death." Portsmouth Herald, October 31, 2013. https://www.seacoastonline.com/story/news/local/york-star/2013/10/31/goat-island-keeper-haunted-light/42059759007/.

A memorable murder in Maine. https://www.seacoastnh.com/a-memorable-mud-er-in-maine/?showall=1.

Why Louis Wagner was Smuttynose Slayer. https://www.seacoastnh.com/History/HistoryMatters/why-louis-wagner-was-smuttynose-slayer/?showall=1.

"Horror on Smuttynose." *Yankee Magazine,* March 1980.

Snow, Edward Rowe. *The Lighthouses of New England.* Beverly, MA: Commonwealth Editions, 2002.

Vaughncottagestarisland. "Who Is the Shoals Pirate Bride Ghost?" Vaughn Cottage, August 26, 2019. https://vaughncottage.wordpress.com/2019/08/26/who-is-the-shoals-pirate-bride-ghost/.

Lighthouse webmaster - Geoffrey Baker - info@lhdigest.com. Lighthouses@Lighthouse digest ... the darker side of Boston Harbor's lighthouses. https://www.lighthousedigest.com/Digest/StoryPage.cfm?StoryKey=863.

"Ghosts of Wood Island - Wood Island Lighthouse." Wood Island Lighthouse - Lighting Saco Bay Since 1806, May 28, 2023. https://woodislandlighthouse.org/about/ghosts-of-wood-island/.

Lighthouse webmaster - Geoffrey Baker - info@lhdigest.com. Lighthouses@lighthouse Digest ... the ghost at Seguin Light Station. https://www.lhdigest.com/Digest/StoryPage.cfm?StoryKey=1143.

"Oct 01, 1945, Page 5 - Sun-Journal at Newspapers.Com." Historical Newspapers from 1700s-2000s - Newspapers.com. https://www.newspapers.com/image/829319677/?match=1&terms=William+P.+Sawyer.

"Matinicus Rock Light: A Ghost behind Closed Doors." NEW ENGLAND FOLKLORE. https://newenglandfolklore.blogspot.com/2015/02/matinicus-rock-light-ghost-behind.html.

"Haunted Lighthouses of the Midcoast." PenBay Pilot. https://www.penbaypilot.com/article/haunted-lighthouses-midcoast/251919.

D'Entremont, Jeremy. *New England Lighthouses: A Virtual Guide.* https://www.newenglandlighthouses.net/.

D'Entremont, Jeremy. *Great Shipwrecks of the Maine Coast.* Beverly, MA: Commonwealth Editions, 2010.

Haunted Lighthouses - Legends and Lore. https://www.hauntedlights.com/haunted2. html.

Lighthouse Digest - America's Lighthouse News & History Magazine." Lighthouse Digest - America's Lighthouse News & History Magazine. https://lighthousedigest.com/.

Noble, Dennis L. *Rescued by the U.S. Coast Guard: Great Acts of Heroism since 1878.* Annapolis, MD: Naval Institute Press, 2005. Google.

Strout, John. "Portland Head Light: A Strout Tradition." The Lighthouse Depot. May 1997. http://www.lighthousedepot.com/lite_digest.asp?action=get_article&sk=170.

"US Lifesaving Service History." U. S. Coast Guard Home Page. https://www.uscg.mil/tcyorktown/Ops/NMLBS/Surf/surf1.asp.

"Wreck of Bark Isadore. Further Particulars." Boston Post, December 5, 1842. https://www.newspapers.com/image/56425094/?match=1&terms=bark%20isadore.

Bales, Jack, and Kenneth Roberts. *Boon Island: Including Contemporary Accounts of the Wreck of the Nottingham Galley*. Hanover [u.a.: Univ. Press of New England, 1996.

Costopoulos, Nina. *Lighthouse Ghosts and Legends*. Birmingham, Ala.: Crane Hill Publishers, 2003.

Lanigan-Schmidt, Therese. *Ghostly Beacons: Haunted Lighthouses of North America*. Atglen, PA: Whitford Press, 2000.

"Legendary Lighthouses: Great Lighthouses-Maine." PBS: Public Broadcasting Service - Portland Head Lighthouse. https://www.pbs.org/legendarylighthouses/html/mainegl.html.

"Legendary Lighthouses: Great Stories-Maine." Owl's Head Lighthouse. https://www.pbs.org/legendarylighthouses/html/mainegs.html#owlshead.

"Legendary Lighthouses: Great Stories-Maine." PBS: Public Broadcasting Service. https://www.pbs.org/legendarylighthouses/html/mainegs.html#boonisland.

"Legendary Lighthouses." PBS: Public Broadcasting Service. https://www.pbs.org/legendarylighthouses.

The New England Lighthouse Storm." John Horrigan Historical Lecture. https://www.historylecture.org/lighthousestorm.html.

Noble, Dennis L. *Lighthouses & Keepers: The U.S. Lighthouse Service and Its Legacy*. Annapolis, MD: Naval Institute Press, 2004.

"Owl's Head Tales." Haunted Lighthouses. https://www.hauntedlights.com/haunted1.html.

"Penfield Reef Lighthouse, Connecticut at Lighthousefriends.com." Lighthouse Friends. https://www.lighthousefriends.com/light.asp?ID=788.

"Boat Wrecks 2." Penobscot Marine Museum, November 1962. https://penobscotmarinemuseum.historyit.com/items/view/digital-collection/196211/gallery.

"Portland Head Lighthouse History." New England Lighthouses: A Virtual Guide - Photos, History, Tours, Cruises, Coastal Accommodations and More. https://lighthouse.cc/portlandhead/history.html.

Roberts, Bruce, and Ray Jones. *New England Lighthouses: Maine to Long Island Sound*. Guilford, CT: Globe Pequot Press, 2005.

"Seguin Island Lighthouse, near Popham Beach, Maine." New England Lighthouses: A Virtual Guide - Photos, History, Tours, Cruises, Coastal Accommodations and More. https://www.lighthouse.cc/seguin/.

The Friends of Seguin Home Page. http://www.seguinisland.org/index.htm.

Bachand, Robert G. *Northeast Lights: Lighthouses and Lightships, Rhode Island to Cape May, New Jersey*. Norwalk, CT: Sea Sports Publications, 1989.

Prospect Harbor Lighthouse. LighthouseFriends. (n.d.). https://www.lighthousefriends.com/light.asp?ID=508

Anderson, Mazie B. "The Ghost of Boston Light." *Yankee Magazine*, October 1998.

"Shot Another, Then Himself." Biddeford-Saco, June 2, 1896.

"Ghosts That Haunt Maine Islands." Boothbay Register. https://www.boothbayregister.com/article/ghosts-haunt-maine-islands/102865.

Kobbe, Gustav. "Life in a Lighthouse."*In Century Magazine*, 365-74. Vol. 47. New York: Century Com, 1894. http://www.scribd.com/doc/32665948/Life-in-a-Lighthouse-Minots-Ledge.

"American Lighthouse Foundation." American Lighthouse Foundation. http://www.lighthousefoundation.org/.

Cahill, Robert Ellis. *Lighthouse Mysteries of the North Atlantic*. Salem, MA: Old Saltbox Pub. House, 1998.

"In Seven Days Duel: Light Keeper Fights Mad Assistant to Save Tower and Life." New-York Tribune, August 11, 1905.

"The Mother Tragedy of the Lonesome Lighthouse." The Virginian-Pilot. September 10, 1922.

Bio and Other Books

Allan Wood is a recently retired college educator who lives near the quaint coast of New Hampshire, and has always held a deep passion for lighthouses and maritime history. As an avid photographer and lifelong New Englander, he has photographed all 168 lighthouse stations in New England and created a comprehensive lighthouse tourism website, NELights.com, to share. Additionally, he has written books and blogs on famous shipwrecks and rescues, hauntings, lighthouse tourism in New England, and historical events involving the largest schooner sailing ships ever built in the early 1900s.

Books to Explore

Lighthouses & Coastal Attractions of
Southern New England:
Connecticut, Rhode Island, and
Massachusetts
ISBN 978-0-7643-5245-4

Lighthouses & Coastal Attractions of
Northern New England:
New Hampshire, Maine, and Vermont
ISBN 978-0-7643-5235-5

Book to Explore

The Rise and Demise
of the
Largest Sailing Ships:
Stories of the Six ansd Seven-Masted
Coal Schooners of New England
ISBN 979-0-3928-3420-4